SARATOGA SPRINGS

SARATOGA SPRINGS

MICHAEL DION

Other Books by Michael Dion:

"Circle of Chance"

"The Music Disc Murder"

ITI Music Corporation

ITI Music Corporation Publishing

16057 Tampa Palms Blvd West

Tampa, FL 33647

Registered with Library of Congress 2018

ISBN: 978-0-9995684-3-9

Printed and bound in the United States

Cover: RoxC LLC/www.roxc.graphics/Roxanne Clapp

Author Photo: Ying (St Peter's Square 2018)

Cover Photo: Canva.com

To My Wife Laura, you allow me the time. Thank you, as I continue on trying to be a better writer. Much Love to You always.

To My Daughter, the mother of two. I can only say have patience and live. I Love You dearly.

Thanks to family and friends once again as I weave my stories.

RIP Art Johnson, my record label partner, writer, musician and friend. You are surely missed.

Saratoga Springs
Chapter 1

Drake Blake had been a respected and effective detective in the town of Saratoga Springs New York, just north of Schenectady. Though from time to time there occurred something out of the ordinary in his 20 years on the force, it was still the summer home of the famous springs for Roosevelt and his family. And if it had not been for the old money which included gangster cash, from years that involved gambling, along with the President, the town would have probably dwindled to nothing over its lifetime.

Befitting a loyal civilian now, the humble citizen Drake resides in the sunshine state of Florida in the lovable town of Marco Island, which is the principal city of Naples.

The Spanish explorers came to the island in the mid-1500s and named the island La Isla de San Marcos meaning Gospel writer St. Mark. But the island itself had been inhabited for over 2000 years, by the Calusa Indians.

During the Civil War, many deserters fled to the island for refuge, where they lived amongst Indians.

During Prohibition, the Syndicate had no trouble with the law so booze poured like water throughout all the clubs that littered the island. After all the resort was the winter resting place for the Syndicate and the law turned its eye since many were on the payroll.

Transiting to a normal life after retirement, Drake had become a greying hair, unshaven and needing a haircut lazy beach-comber, who found his way on a train back to Saratoga to help out on old colleague.

D.B. as his very close friends called him, though there are only a few, hated to fly and other than driving his 1972 Mustang, he always took the train and in particular a sleeper even if it was a short distance.

Drake found the comfort of the trains and old attendants the last of the classic age of travelling. "It's here where you can talk or not talk to another person, kind of like being in a bar or tavern", Drake commented.

Lamenting to his self he thought, "Sometimes the acquaintances last forever, and sometimes they last for the day or night and then they are gone. Just a moment in time."

His Mustang, a Mach 1 was bought brand new after his discharge and retirement. A type of muscle car painted in the Ford blue grabber color with a black diamond shape hood. It was his prize attachment.

At 52 and unmarried, Drake had become a lethargic sleuth of some nature, only taking jobs when it suited him and for his closest friends and a few enemies after they served their time for a crime committed. In fact, some of his best clients were former criminals.

Yesterday he was sitting on his favorite chaise, feet propped up on his deck, reading the "dailies at Aqueduct, Springs, Los Alamitos, Del Mar and the Golden Gate, all the while peering out at the sand, the water and the few people strolling along the walkway. This was in his opinion the best time of the year, winter when it was 72 degrees and sunny.

Muttering out loud on the deck he said, "Tomorrow, I'll be onward and upward back to the northern tundra in wintertime, freezing my ass off. I truly no longer miss the cold. Must be my age", he chuckled.

In 1973, Amtrak took over the old D & H Railroad to allow the company to expand its stops past the Springs all the way to St. Albans, the last stop before Canada.

Drake was happy about the extension since he hated waiting at airports. He thought it was more like a bus terminal, hoping on a plane that acted as a giant transporter to travel. He was sure he would never change his feelings. For him, it was either a train ride or driving his own car.

So on this overcast February day, Drake boarded the train finding his cabin in the fourth car where he sat himself down after hanging up his sparse clothes of a black winter jacket, scarf and his grey suit coat. His black shoes hadn't seen polish in months, while he sat in the sun on the beach in his old Hawaiian shirt, shorts and flip-flops. And his winter wear hadn't been worn in over a year, but he was still able to fit in them since he did take exercising seriously particularly at this stage of his life.

When he was in his 20's and 30's, he weighed 165 and though after retirement he drifted upwards to 180, his running, weightlifting and walking regime thanks to his lady friend at the local gym, helped him to stay somewhat healthy, in spite of his several steaks and whiskey on a weekly basis.

Passing by Jacksonville and seeing the Army transports loading up dockside, sent Drake's memory of his long-lost love when he was in Nam and she was a nurse.

Hilary Westingham came from that high society akin to the old money that made New England and Northern New

York famous for lawn parties, polo and brief but exciting summers before the spectacular colors of the Fall and the blizzards of the winter.

Hilary had dark hair and dark eyes who after receiving approval from her parents enlisted in the Army to help the "boys" in Viet Nam. A graduate from Princeton, engaged to another socialite from Boston, she had everything the world could offer, yet she couldn't sit still and be a home wife for anyone. Some of her classmates referred to her as the reincarnation of Amelia Earhart, being the daredevil for almost anything. So Hilary decided that helping others was her way of slowing down a bit and contributing to society.

Back in '68, Drake was an Army Major reservist, and all but ready to retire when the war recalled him to duty even at the ripe old age of 47. There at Tripler Medical Hospital in Hawaii, Drake met Hilary. She was all of 30, much younger than he but they hit it off.

He'd been shot up pretty bad during the Cambodian Excursion in May 1970, when the 1st Cav invaded Cambodia. The Cav had settled down in the field with reporters on board, where Drake led his backup company coming under fire that lasted all day till they were rescued. However, by that time he and another officer from his Battalion, the 12th Cav, suffered extreme wounds.

With his injured almost unusable left arm, it took twelve hours to get fly Drake back to a U.S. facility. There the medics at Tripler were able to place stints and metal pieces into his arm so that it functioned almost perfectly.

After his operation and the treatments started, Hilary who was the head nurse at the time, began to strike up a mischievous close relationship with Drake. Some of his ward buddies called it "kismet", but Drake called it the laws of attraction.

Several months later before being returned to the front in Da Nang, Hilary and Drake had an affair. Not planned and certainly out of character for both of them, they decided that no one should know about it, but Hilary's best friend and roommate on base knew everything about it and kept her silence.

Rachel McPherson, also 30, was originally from Oswego, but her family moved to Saratoga Springs when she was six.

Because she came from a military family, Rachel decided to enlist and help out in the Viet Nam War, since her Uncle had been a great influence in her life having spent time onboard an aircraft carrier during the Second World War. Wanting to be a nurse, she enlisted in the Army and graduated on the fast track since they were short of medical personnel in the field.

Shortly afterwards, Rachel was sent directly to Nam and was bunked up with Hilary, where they became fast friends and sisters on a mission.

After the short-lived affair with Drake, as he was still recovering well, Hilary requested to be transferred to Hue, in South Vietnam. There she could assist in the recovery of those US troops. Rachel on the other hand, was requested by Hilary to stay behind and keep tabs on Drake.

After returning to the front, unknown to Drake at that time, Hilary was only 99 km away, about 60 miles when disaster struck on an afternoon filled with much celebration.

There, the Hawaiian National Guard and sailors from two cruisers were having a party, when the base was overrun with Cong and Hilary was killed along with several doctors, nurses and other wounded personnel.

After the frantic calls for help came through Central Command, reinforcements to the base were late in arriving. The irony about this incident was that Hue was never overrun again. It was a freak occurrence.

Drake who had continued to write to Hilary never heard a response and only found out about her death six months after the fact when he and his Battalion were sent up to the area to be the next in line to support the base.

When he learned of her death, he wept for a long time. He vowed to never again be that attached to anyone.

As heavy rains pelted the train as it rattled from side to side, bringing Drake back to reality. He settled in his cabin room and began to read the book he had been reading for what seemed to be a lifetime, Jack London's "A Daughter of the Snows". London's story was about a strong woman living in the Yukon who was torn between two suitors.

Every time Drake started to read the book something would come up and he'd have to put it down and then start all over when he had the time. This seemed to be the right time again.

Subconsciously, the book reminded him of Hilary.

"Perhaps" he thought, "This is why I can never finish it!"

Clickity clack, clickity clack, the sound put Drake asleep but then woke him up around 2 am. He was amazed that he slept sitting in the chair, since the attendant did not wake him to turn the bed down, but rather placed the blanket over Drake in order to not disturb him.

After relieving himself, Drake returned to put together the bed and climbed into it and immediately fell back to sleep listening to the sounds of the train.

Traveling by rail from Fort Meyers to Saratoga would normally take about 35 hours, making several stops along the way including Tampa, Savannah and New York City.

His closest friend, Army Buddy and now fellow police chief Sam Thackery had called Drake about a missing girl from a family that both men had known for years. In fact, her dad was the Fire Chief in the town, and Army Buddy who was part of their group during the War.

Her mom had passed away several years prior from a bone disease that couldn't be treated in spite of the "Springs natural powers."

Ashley, the daughter had been born later in the lives of Teresa and Bill Mathews and was now 20. Bill at 52 was forced to retire due to a back injury carrying a local woman, Doris Stein, twice his weight, out of a burning building.

Bill, Sam and Drake were together in Nam, having all been recalled to active duty to serve in the Military Police. And while Bill was a fireman, the Army brought him in as a "fire expert and bomb squad operator".

Though all three men were now retired from the Army, Sam was the only one still drawing a steady paycheck from the city.

Life seemed to be normal with Ashley attending Skidmore College, the local private liberal arts school where she was studying Dance and Theater, in hopes of performing on Broadway.

In her junior year she worked part time at the bookstore on campus. With a class size of between 10 to 15 students, she enjoyed close attention from her instructors for her curriculum.

Drake thought it very suspicious that her Dad didn't call him first but it had been years since they last spoke, and decided not to take it personally, since he didn't live there anymore.

Curiously, the Chief was somewhat concerned that it had been three days after she went missing that Bill called him and asked for help. Further to the weirdness was that there was no ransom note nor phone call demanding anything.

For the Springs, it was a strange case indeed, particularly since the "forefathers" of the community had cleaned up most of the crime along with the members of various criminal organizations years ago. Yet, there did remain some deeply planted families with ties that went to Chicago, New York and to Florida that seemed to never go away and still controlled much of the "action" in the Springs.

Even when Drake was the primary detective for the city, no matter how many times he thought that he eradicated the Syndicate, up popped another member with major ties to the Albany government, New York City or elsewhere.

"Never ending it was, stomping out another bug", Drake would say.

Saratoga Springs
Chapter 2

In the morning, Drake found himself getting close to Washington D.C. After taking the standard cramped quick shower, he dressed and headed to the galley car for breakfast of eggs, bacon and toast with coffee and orange juice.

The porter remembered Drake from years gone by and bid him to sit down in a booth by himself. Drake was happy to oblige so he wouldn't have to carry on some small talk that led to nowhere.

The porter approached the table and said, "Mr. Blake, right?"

Drake smiled and said, "Yep you remembered, why it's been several years since I was last on this train, how could you...".

The porter cut him off quickly and replied, "Mr. Blake, I never forgot someone who helped me the last time we were together. You helped me with my sis', when she was having a go at it in The Springs. But she OK now and straight, which I am overjoyed that you helped me in doin' this for her. I never forget you sir!"

Drake smiled and felt so honored it brought a tear to his eye. He couldn't recall being that choked up over anyone before in his life, except Hilary.

He thanked the old porter as he bowed leaving to fetch Drake's breakfast.

When the train arrived in D.C., Drake was able to step off and call the Chief.

Sam told Drake that no one had contacted Bill as of yet and they still had no leads as to where she might have been taken. All they knew was that she was working at the Bookstore after her classes last week on Friday. After that there is no sign of her. She never returned to her room and her roommate never heard from her.

Drake pondered over a few possibilities of what may have happened. The sad part in these situations is that the victim ends up dead. Many times a family member is involved or an ex-boyfriend. However, in rare cases it is someone all together unknown.

After getting back on the train, Drake began to get antsy. Perhaps he should have flown instead, but he needed the time to refocus himself into standard police investigations and shake off the sand and lifestyle of a beach bum.

As the train passed through New York City, he knew it was a just a short time now to his final destination and he'd be there to assist and hopefully find Ashley alive.

Saratoga Springs, known for its mineral water, was also known for off track betting, Meyer Lansky and of course the racetracks. And not necessary in that order. Plus, the three of these intrinsic things intersected with each other over and over many, many years.

The history of "The Springs" is jaded at best with the state and city forefathers being the greatest appalling culprits that almost killed off the entire area by opening and closing down the gambling houses that resided mostly along the lakefront. At one time, the Grand Union Hotel, was touted as the largest in the world when it was originally built. Lansky and others lost a ton of money when the leaders of the government decided to clean up the city. Somehow, and in spite of their deranged bumbling in this effort, it recovered over time, but slowly, keeping the rift raft away but allowing some old money families to flourish.

In the new age of high society, it became the "Newport" of New York, with exclusive summertime parties of the rich, horse racing, gambling and polo.

It was also famous for the invention of the potato chip, or at least that's the legend, though no one knows for sure.

A sacred place for the Mohawk and other Native Americans, believing that the natural bubbly water had been moved by Manitou, bestowing it with healing properties. (Manitou was akin to the Iroquois Orenda, the divine and essential force of life amongst the Algonquians). Its ideas were ever present in everything, even if the Dutch, British and French all took their turns hosting their flags over the town throughout its early years.

Over time, the railroad and the hotels that dotted the mineral springs took over where the Indians once relaxed and bathed their own troubles away.

Throughout a century and half, "summer cottages", or mansions of the rich scattered the landscape. Besides, Roosevelt, other famous attendees of the Springs had included composer Victor Herbert, politician Daniel Webster, women's rights activist Susan B. Anthony, opera singer Caruso, Irish playwright and poet Oscar Wilde, actress Sarah Bernhardt, and patriotic march composer John Philip Sousa.

Originally born in Saratoga Springs, Drake's dad was a groomsman for the race track, while his mom was a stay at home and part time school teacher. Drake grew up around the stables, the thugs and the money that controlled the community.

Drake had just become a police officer for the town when World War II got going and was initially not accepted because of his police duties. In 1945, with the needs of the War, he eventually was called up to be part of the Military Police in France as a 1St Lieutenant.

Even the once mighty and charming Springs fell into a depression as the war effort ramped up, with gas rationing and casino's and hotels shutting down. Yet the Syndicate didn't pull back as they opened the Raceway and Gaming in 1941 that not only had slot machines, but also included horse harness racing. There were now two families that controlled the town's gambling.

Sonny Cohen from Boston owned and operated the Raceway and belonged to the Massachusetts Family. Ironically his business competed with Florida's Moe Abramson's major Racetrack for six weeks each year, but then controlled the attention of the locals and those wishing to gamble away their money. No matter, the Syndicate continued to make money even with the lack of business during the WWII.

Though Sonny made more all year long, it couldn't compete with the prestige or the overall winnings that Moe made in those six short weeks each year.

More fame and money grabbed the attention in 1972 at Preakness and Belmont Park, where one horse seemed to stand out amongst the many, Secretariat. His nickname was Big Red because of his chestnut color and stood taller and weighed more than other thoroughbred horses.

The Syndicate had their sights on the new favorite but decided to run their own horses and made several deals to run them along side of the celebrity horse. They also moved their horses into the northeast to train and get them ready for the following summer. These stables belonged to Bill Williams, where he was paid handsomely for attending to the thoroughbreds.

Because Sonny wanted Moe's track, he was banking on the three different ways to make money: The track itself, the horses and the off track betting. It was a winner's paradise if he could pull it off.

Moe on the other hand wasn't ready to sell it to Sonny but was willing to share it if the price was right. The dilemma that it created for the Families was neither pleasant or in the best interest, as it would entail cutting Allen Stein out of the picture completely.

Because Allen was very good friends with the Miami Family, this would cause a serious situation if he was not laundering the money for the Families. Several discussions and side conversations involving a possible "hit" on Sonny continued amongst the heads of the Families without a definite decision.

Sonny was generally known as a hot head who like his adopted son, Danny Stein, was impatient with whatever he was into at that moment. He had swayed Danny to abduct Ashley in order to convince the Florida Family to back his desire to take over Moe's racetrack, but in the end that plan backfired and he denied ever advising the Stein kid to do such a thing.

The Tampa Family was livid with Sonny and asked that he be warned of his misgivings, since it was adding unnecessary attention to all of the Families, including Boston. Miami Camp decided to let it ride believing that Sonny would come around and relax his desires and continue to just be. Yet, Tampa had other ideas and was vying for an imprint in New York. So Giuseppe and Juan were sent to the Springs to monitor the situation with Sonny and any recourse that should be taken.

Saratoga Springs
Chapter 3

After the War, Drake stayed in the Army reserves and
returned to the Springs.

As a decorated veteran, he was immediately promoted to
Detective, due to his service and his time already spent as a
policeman.

Unaware that Rachel had returned to the Springs, after her
discharge, Drake met up with her again since she was
working as the hotel concierge at the Adelphi.

Drake's new position allowed him the opportunity to meet
several key members of society especially during the
summer lawn parties. With the wide open porches at some
of the hotels it became the place for social scenes and
political gatherings that unfolded nightly. It was where
those that wanted to be seen, be influential, meet and
circulate. Business deals and afternoon excursions along
the lake were common, that virtually appeared to be out of
the musical "My Fair Lady".

As the years went by one woman took charge of rebuilding
Saratoga Springs into the prim and proper society location
it was today. Her name was Marylou Whitney. She
worked to rebuild and change the way people and
organizations looked at the Springs. And of course, this
included the racetrack, the annual Fair and to some degree
the gambling that still continued in the backrooms of the
city.

Whether it was prestige or money, famous and infamous
people lined the streets during each and every summer.

Aaron Copeland in 1930 composed first major work for solo piano followed by another in 1932.

Then there was Meyer Lansky, whose first project in the Springs was the Piping Rock. Originally known as the "Syndicate's Accountant", he was instrumental arranging and brokering deals even amongst the government. During WWII, this included the Office of Naval Intelligence. He partnered with Frank Costello and Joe Adonis and were protected by the local politicians to maintain the casino. Eventually Meyer was sentenced to a short jail time for his gambling efforts in the Springs, but it didn't stop the money from flowing.

As a police officer, Drake never took a dime from any of the politicians or criminal racketeering that went on in the Springs. He was the most honest cop on the beat and sometimes paid for his honesty by not being invited to certain events or functions. But it never bothered him, since he was kept busy enough with the other wrongdoings being committed throughout Saratoga.

Nor as a Detective, was he worried about locking up some of Lansky's men, even when his boss warned him and then looked the other way.

Always an inconsistency of contradictions, since the Syndicate helped patrol the harbors for the Navy during World War II, the Feds would arrest some of the bosses and/or deport them soon after their assistance.

Drake in his own way, did the same, which wasn't always a smartest thing to do, as his boss would tell him. So, it kept him on his toes, frequently looking over his shoulder, just in case.

Saratoga Springs
Chapter 4

As the train approached Saratoga, Drake's heart skipped a
beat, since this would be the first chance he visited his
hometown after his parents had passed away.

He had decided to stay in one of the oldest hotels called the
Adelphi, where Rachel once worked. They had lost contact
and though he wondered whatever happened to her, he
never pursued it.

The Adelphi was a much smaller yet impressive hotel that
once upon a time rivaled the "Grand" for its suites. Unlike
most of the other hotels that fell on hard times over the
years, the Adelphi maintained itself like it did in its once
magnificent and decadent style. Overstuffed chairs and
couches lined the lobby in ornate fashion. It was like
stepping back in time.

When the train pulled into the station, Sam was waiting for
him on the platform as he stepped off into the afternoon
heat of the Adirondacks. February days when it wasn't
snowing would reach into the 60's, while the night air
would drop into the 20's.

Drake thought, "It won't be long before the chill of the
night air blanketed the town with fur coats covering up the
rich and the poor alike".

Smiling at each other, Sam walked straight up to Drake and
said, "Christ, long time, nice to see you again. And Thanks
for coming to help out your old friend!"

"Sam", Drake replied, "Anytime, we go way back, and if I
can help, I will."

Driving into town the two old comrades conversed in only small talk, as Sam wanted to wait until Drake got settled in, before giving him the lowdown about the case.

After checking into the hotel, Drake and the bell captain walked up to his room. Hanging up his shirts, he then stored his other clothes and laid out his toiletries before he headed back downstairs to meet up with Sam. When he reached the bottom floor, which was two floors below his room, he wasn't watching where he was walking and bumped into a woman, who dropped some papers on the floor.

Looking at her, he stammered a bit and then said, "Well, I'll be damned, Rachel, how the hell are you?"

Surprised and taken back by seeing her long-standing friend, Rachel responded. "Drake Blake, the years have been kind to you, it must be the Florida living. No cold weather, just sunshine and mojito's, I suppose."

Drake, started to chuckle and replied, "Yes and no, I suppose. But Rachel, you are still stunning. What are you doing here?"

"Well, I run this place now, as it seems to be one of the few places to stay town and since you didn't marry me, I ran off to the South to find a man and got hitched. Now though, I had to do something with my time, so..."

"But I thought you got married", Drake said.

Rachel smiled and said, "Yep, but Sandy passed away a little over two years ago and since this was his family's hotel, I inherited the 'old lady', as she is called these days. Sandy was from Tennessee, where his family owned

18

Gathers Whiskey, along with a few other hotels across the country.

The family sent Sandy and I here to run the business and then sold it to Sandy and I for almost nothing, knowing how downtrodden it was at the time. Sandy and I dreamt big and decided to go for it and revamped the old hotel into something spectacular, I must say, but he died before seeing how it was going to change. Now it's all mine and I am keeping the promise to keep her afloat in a manner that is befitting."

Just as Sam was approaching them, Drake scratched his forehead said, "Wow, this is so incredible."

Sam quipped, "Oh I forgot to mention that Rachel was here to you as we drove in, sorry!"

"No problem Sam. It must have been dumb luck for me to bump into her. It has been a very long time. And yep, old Sam here has asked me to help him with something, but I'd like to get together and catch up some more if you have the time?"

Rachel responded, "Anytime. I live here so it's easy to get a hold of me. Just leave word at the front desk and someone will find me. For now, I've got to go see Mrs. Darling. She apparently has lost her dog or something."

Then Rachel smiled, shifted herself towards Drake and kissed him on the cheek and said, "Later you." And with that she headed up the ornate stairs covered in the red, blue and gold floral carpet.

Chuckling to himself, Drake couldn't believe his luck. Rachel and he might have become a couple following

Hilary's death and his recovery. They had become very close, but more than timing, both of them knew nothing would come of it, particularly during those years.

Following the War, Drake realized that the police academy would put a damper on his soliciting Rachel, along with the fact that she came from a well to do family. And while his Dad worked her family's stables, coming from opposite sides of that social fence, didn't help them flirting with the idea.

Smiling, Sam woke Drake out of his romanticizing and reminiscing as he said, "Ready? I want to go by the station first to give you all the information that we have collected so far."

Drake, then said, "Yep, let's go."

Saratoga Springs
Chapter 5

As Drake walked back into the station house, it really was "Deja vu". Little had changed since he was last here. The only thing new was the larger than life "white board", hanging in the main room, while almost all of the same people sat at their assigned desks.

Millie, the station "Mom" walked up to Drake with an ear to ear grin and wrapped her arms around him. She was only five feet one and appeared smaller than he remembered.

After all Drake was five eleven, so no doubt his stature was much more defined after leaving the job years ago, and not being around this short woman.

After refamiliarizing himself with the place and the people he sauntered into Sam's office where he was surprised by the photos and arrows on a board indicating Ashley and where she might be.

Sam was able to figure out that after her shift had ended at 6PM at the bookstore, she left to go meet up with some friends at Dutton's, the local coffee shop.

It was only three blocks from the bookshop so Ashley would have more than likely walked there but vanished and never met up with her group.

Further investigations concluded after speaking with Millie. She had spoken with Ashley's roommate, who indicated that she had been troubled by the constant harassment from Danny Stein, who had attended Skidmore and recently graduated with a degree in business.

Danny Stein was the godson of an infamous gangster that was able to become wealthy in the Springs by associating himself with the Meyer Lansky organization in Florida.

Danny, though not a criminal or gangster by trade, was nonetheless a "know it all" and loud mouth, who tried to run the College like it was his for the taking.

Though no charges were ever brought against Danny, he remained someone that the police had monitored as best as they could, given the circumstances that some of the politicians were still in the back pockets of the criminal families in the Springs.

As best as Sam could surmise, there was some sort of confrontation between Danny and Ashley as she made her way to meeting her friends.

Allegedly, there was a friend of hers, Judy, that drove by as Ashley was being held tightly, almost violently by Danny and then shoved into a car, before speeding out into the street, almost smashing into Judy's car.

Judy was sure that neither Danny nor the driver saw her as they peeled away from the curb.

From that moment on, there had been no sign of Ashley and or Danny and the police are quite worried about her life.

Her Dad, Bill, visited the Stein house to follow up on this lead but apparently got nowhere in his conversation with the butler. Likewise, the police didn't get much further and no one has seen or heard from either Danny or Ashley since that night.

Hence Sam was perplexed since he felt that he was in a pickle at not finding Ashley nor anything else about the case.

Upon hearing the story, Drake asked if Sam had gone to visit Stein. Sam said "No!"

So that afternoon Drake and Sam agreed to drive over to the Stein house and to monitor their actions to see if they could shed some light on Ashley's whereabouts.

The Stein Mansion was on Clinton St, about 100 yards from the Annandale Mansion and down the street from the Union Gables Inn.

Doris and Allen Stein, parents to their only son, Danny, were originally from Russia but grew up in New York City.

Allen's name was Steinberg but changed it when he immigrated to America in 1902. With the help of his old friend, now living in Florida, and his own Father, he was able to open a clothing store primarily catering to the wealthy because of the materials used as fabrics in manufacturing both men and women's clothes. Interesting enough, even during World War II, when fabric was hard to come by, The Stein Haberdashery always had what anyone wanted.

Because of his association, Allen's store acted as a money laundering location for off-track betting, as repayment for advancing Allen the loan to start up the store. It was profitable for Allen and The Families while making the Stein couple and their son affluent members of the community.

Danny was afforded a luxury charmed life, who took advantage of this and seemed to always be in a pickle of some sort, knowing that his family could wrangle him out of any troubling circumstances he was in.

After the briefing, Drake decided to go back to the hotel and "listen to the walls" in the hotel lobby. That night after eating alone, he was able to pick up some chatter regarding Danny from a young woman at the bar. She was discussing of all things his private parts with another friend as they continued to throw back Tequila shooters. It seemed that Danny was a wild child with the women of the town and wasn't afraid if anyone knew about his manhood.

Just as they were about to leave two large men in oversized business suits and dusters, walked up to the girls and asked them if they wanted to party. The girls both smiled, and the redhead said, "Only if you know who is there. I'd like some action tonight!"

The men didn't blink but assured them that he would be there for their pleasure. And with that, all four left the bar.

Drake was debating if he should follow them, when Rachel appeared out of nowhere and side tracked his attention.

Looking lovely as ever, she said, "Hey there DB, what are you up to?"

Drake cussed under his breathe, as he stood up and replied, "Oh I was just on my way out to get some fresh air, care to join me?"

As Rachel began to respond she said, "Oh, I am sorry, maybe another time, I am frantically being waved at by my assistant. I will catch up with you later." Then Rachel walked off.

Drake then deciding to follow the four, sprinted to the doorway looking outside and caught a glimpse of the four-door limo, with the license plate "Stein2" printed on it. Not having a car to his own, he saw a taxi sitting across the street and dashed to the stand, knocked on the window and asked, "Are you for hire?"

The cabbie looked stunned, turning to face Drake with a mouth full of food from the sandwich he had just bitten into, and said, "Ya man, but I get off in a half an hour."

"OK", said Drake, realizing the cabbie was Jamaican from his accent, as he stepped in the back of the taxi and said, "Follow that limo that just left the hotel!"

With that, the cabbie placed his sandwich next to him on the aluminum foil and peeled out of the space and made a u-turned but did as Drake instructed him by staying several car lengths behind the Cadillac with the special license plate, as it drove through town at the posted speed limit.

The cabbie followed the limo onto Union Ave out past Gilbert Corners continuing on Union to the Lake, where there was a boat ramp with docks and a large yachts tied up at one end.

The limo had driven down to the one where the yacht was and stopped while the cabbie, as directed pulled alongside the upper road that was above the marina.

In the dark, but under the dock lights, Drake could see a two door dark green Ford parked with a logo that included a horse and slot machine in a circle. Drake was a bit familiar with it but decided to ask the cabbie if he knew who the car belonged to?

"Da man, it is Sonny Cohen's car. He da only one dat have dat color."

Opening the limo door, four people scrambled out and climbed aboard the very large wooden yacht that looked like it belonged to President Roosevelt that flew a flag with a blue and white crest of an ox. Unfamiliar with who it might belong to he asked the cabbie.

"Breddah, Oh dat Mr. Stein's boat. Suh yuh nah guh badda guh", (So, you are not going to bother going), the cabbie chirped. "He own da Stein Haberdashery which originally was for men only but Mrs. Stein introduced women's wear years ago and the store is probably a gold mine, since it caters to only the most affluent people in town and in New York, Chicago and Miami."

Drake was floored that the cabbie knew so much and said to him, "No I am just checking on them and by the way, how do you know all that?"

"It's easy mate", he said. "Yuh keep yuh nose to the ground, yuh ears wide open and yuh mouth shut and da peoples in this ride seh weh yuh feel fi she (will say anything), even if day think yuh ain't dehyah..."

Drake was amused and astounded by this information and the cabbie's attitude. Then he told him that he could return to town and thanked him for the night ride.

That evening unbeknownst to Drake the two girls on the boat had partied with Danny, after the goons locked up

Ashley. When he was done, the goons took the girls back to the hotel so they could get a ride home.

Ashley had heard the conversation between the four men and Danny, talking about the papers detailing the burning of the buildings that she saw after the fire and the merging of the two racetracks. She didn't know what to make of it all, but knew she was in trouble.

Afterwards, as instructed by Sonny, the two guys went back to the yacht, found Danny asleep in the "captains' chair" placed tape over his mouth and tied him up, since he was trying to fight them off.

When he wouldn't stop moving, Juan punched him straight in the face and knocked him out.

Giuseppe stepped over to the dials on the bridge and fired up the engines by pushing a button. Juan was busy on the dock untying the lines from the cleats.

Stepping into the dingy that was tied up next to the yacht, Juan pulled the engine cord a few times to start the motor. After sputtering a few times, the engine started and Juan crept away from the dock towards the yacht now slowly moving towards the center of the lake.

Upon figuring that this was a good spot, Giuseppe shut the engines off of the STEIN1, where it stopped and began to lower its anchors to latch onto the bottom.

When the dingy finally arrived at the same spot as the yacht, Giuseppe called out, almost silently to Juan, to tie the big boat to the nearby buoy, for additional support.

After the support line was in place, Giuseppe shut everything down except for the power generator. He then took the keys and anything else needed to restart the yacht.

Walking into the lower galley and hallway, Giuseppe located Ashley's cabin, unlocked it and found her asleep. Going back on deck he untied Danny who was still out from Juan's punch and placed him in an empty cabin on a bed.

Back up topside, Giuseppe double checked himself and then walked over to the side of the yacht and climbed down the outside ladder unto the dingy and the two goons quietly slipped away not leaving any exits for the couple after they awoke.

Saratoga Springs
Chapter 6

The next morning Drake met with Sam for breakfast at the
hotel and gave Sam his report of the prior night's activity.
Sam said, to Drake, "Why didn't you call me for back up or
go on the boat yourself?"

Drake was smiling, "Nope, not yet. We still need to dig
around and find out what else is going on. Besides, if the
women don't show back up, then it's your case and time to
slap handcuffs on the goons."

Afterwards Sam drove Drake over to the station where he
loaned him an unmarked Plymouth Fury to drive while he
was in town.

Leaving the station, Drake decided to return to the hotel
and speak with Rachel about the two girls who were at the
bar during the prior night.

Finding Rachel in her office, Drake sat down and explained
why he was there, which Rachel reacted sadly to. She
didn't know that Ashley had disappeared but heard some
discussions from her staff about a girl being shoved into a
car about a week ago. However, she thought it was some
lovers quarrel and nothing to really get involved with.
Now that Drake told her that it was Bill's kid that went
missing, Rachel became very concerned, particularly since
no one had seen her since.

Asking Rachel about the incident that occurred at the bar,
Rachel was able to tell Drake who the two women were.
Both worked at the Stein Women's Boutique and probably
had come into contact with Danny at one of his thrashy
parties.

Drake, asked, "Thrashy?"

"Yeah", responded Rachel. "They are usually loud, with music and fireworks and pretty much a free for all sex feast by the time it is all over."

Drake cracked a grin and asked, "How do you know that?"

"Well, now that you asked", Rachel responded with a grin.

"When Sandy was alive, we were invited to many parties and so we decided to be a good neighbor and community peer and attend one of these shindigs. As it turned out, by about midnight we were looking at each other as most of the young men and women had shed their clothes and began having sex all over the inside of the house and grounds where the pool and tennis court were located. Needless to say, Sandy and I just boogied out of their and didn't say much to each other until the next day."

Rachel went on. "Look I am not a prude, but it was like a hippie fest or something, that neither of us were comfortable with. I prefer my intimacy intimate."

"Okay" replied Drake. "But was there anything else going on that you could remember, like who was there and did you see or hear anything unusual?"

Rachel cracked half a smile, "Well, there are French doors that open out unto the grounds and during the initial hour or so after we had arrived, Danny and several friends per se, where adjourned in the room facing the grounds. I couldn't tell you what was said, but the Mayor, and several of our town's commissioners were seated in the overstuffed chairs, as Danny was standing there, berating some Italian looking fellow and some girl. Sandy was a bit taken back by it and so we moved away from the doors and headed inside to the living room. About fifteen minutes later all those people joined us there along with the guy and girl. I could see that the girl had a bruise on the left side of her mouth and the guy's forehead had a black mark on one side. To me it appeared that they had both been smacked around. But no one spoke about it."

Drake seemed perplexed and asked, "Do you know who they were, the girl and guy?"

"Not at that moment, but later we did find out that they were Danny's cousin and girlfriend, but never saw them again", Rachel said.

"So, Danny Stein has a temper?" asked Drake.

"Oh yes, a terrible one", replied Rachel.

"Well then, do you think that he was dating or involved with Ashley", asked Drake.

"Perhaps", answered Rachel. "He liked younger women, especially college girls, and in spite of Bill and Teresa's upbringing, she could have been taken in by his looks and his bad-boy panache."

Drake said, "Look Rachel, I need for you to start asking around if your staff and anyone else might know what has happened here. My main concern is the abduction but since no one has asked for ransom, it could be that she found out something about what Danny was up to and he decided that he couldn't take a chance and so he grabbed her to keep her quiet."

"Geez, I hope this isn't true", replied Rachel.

She continued, "You see, Bill had to retire because he carried Doris Stein from the original Woman's boutique shop that the Stein couple had purchased. Unfortunately she was twice his weight and she was in the attic when the fire took the building down. Both Allen and Doris were thankful for his courage, but never did anything to help him or his family afterwards. So, there is some bad blood there, even though Danny had kind of dated Ashley, when she was a Freshman. But I think it was to make sure that Bill didn't nose around or do anything."

"Really" said Drake. "This kidnapping could be over some past incident and nothing more?"

Rachel squeezed Drake's hand and said, "You forget, anything is possible in the old Indian mineral Springs!"

Saratoga Springs
Chapter 7

In a place not far from Drake's home in Florida, there was a connection that overshadowed the Springs. The Tampa Mafia along with their Cigar trade, had been linked to Cuba that existed since the early 1900's.

Though the "Syndicate" had been instrumental and notorious in the cities of New York, Chicago, New Orleans, Los Angeles, and Cleveland, Tampa was in fact, a major player in the underworld of drugs, prostitution and gambling.

Italian Giuseppe D'Angelo and Cuban Juan Lopez Montez were raised in Ybor City, where a blend of the two nationalities lived and survived in the broken-down houses of fishermen and laborers.

Outside in the back to back alley, the two boys learned to be friends playing children games, speaking in a made-up language that only the two could understand. There they befriended each other throughout their teen years into their early adulthood, as they became the muscle behind the reigning Family that controlled the city and elsewhere.

Tied to primarily Chicago and Miami, the two men answered to the Tampa Boss but found themselves in Saratoga Springs or New York at any time performing a task that no one else would dare to do. The two friends took on any and all jobs that Tampa wanted to complete.

Sometimes this was to scare someone into selling property or the guys would torch a car or even a building to make the point. Regrettably, this also included on occasion the hanging of someone just to make sure that it was understood, who was in control.

When it was suggested by Miami to go to Saratoga to assist in a situation, the two men got on the next plane and did as they were told.

Both men were almost six feet tall with black hair and black eyes. They were the "enforcers" used to control anything for Tampa or Miami. Threat or death made no difference. They were not afraid to do anything that was asked of them.

Arriving at a prescribed hour they were received by the Stein driver, Anthony Romano.

Anthony had been part of the Tampa family but was moved to the Springs by the Boss to keep tabs on the businesses that the Allen and Doris laundered.

After picking Giuseppe and Juan up from the airport, the three men rehashed their lives in Ybor, as they headed for the Adelphi Hotel, where Drake was spending his time.

It should be noted that when the two men travelled to Saratoga, it was at the invitation of both Allen and Doris to help out a minor problem that could have a potential major impact on any one of the Families, or so Allen told the Florida connection. This caused Tampa and Miami to take immediate control of the situation to make sure nothing led itself back to the Families.

Danny Stein, had by his own choice kidnapped the daughter of the prior Fire Chief over something incidental and stupid, that now had landed on the front doors of the Syndicate.

It seems that as a teenager, Ashley would sometimes tag along with her Dad to look at a burnt out building after a fire, so that she could search through the rubble to see what she could find.

Being a Dad, Bill would explain certain things to her, like never place your sweater to dry on a heater or never smoke in bed, because this is what might happen.

This time however, when they went to the Stein Boutique blackened shop, they found what looked like a bottle of bleach and a fire cap that appeared to be an incendiary device.

Harmlessly in another room, Ashley found an open safe that had some papers in it detailing what should be done after a fire in dealing with the insurance company. It also included several more buildings in town that would be destroyed by quite a few methods, and the names of contacts in Florida on both coasts to be contacted.

After reading the documents, she took them to her Dad who later discussed whatever was in these papers with Allen directly and turned them over to him, as to avoid any additional involvement.

Allen of course denied any wrongdoings to the Chief and because the family was part of the high society in town, there was never any charges brought against them.

Unfortunately, Bill had mentioned to the Allen that Ashley had found them in an open box, which put Ashley in the middle of knowing something that she should not have.

By the time Drake had pieced together the connection of Ashley to Danny and the underworld organizations, he knew that it was just a matter of time before she would disappear for good, if all of this was true.

Luckily Rachel informed Drake that two gangster looking guys from Florida had checked into her hotel.

Then working with Sam, they developed a plan to look in the goon's room for anything that could lead them to Ashley and what else they might be up to.

Two nights following the night the party girls went on the boat, Giuseppe and Juan Lopez decided to dine in the hotel and left their room to head downstairs. Being the macho types, they were joking and decided to see who could run the fastest to the bottom. Now granted they were on the fourth floor which was too far to run, but the stairs were built in a square fashion with the elevators in the middle. So, turning the corners at high speed would entail some immaculate grace, which neither of these overgrown boys had. Nonetheless they started to run…

While they were claiming who was number one, Drake had been notified by Rachel that they were now downstairs in the dining room. He knew that it was now or never, so he walked up to their room to rummage through it in hopes of finding out more about their operation or direction.

Looking through the closets and drawers, Drake went about his business.

Sam as the police chief, couldn't condone his actions, but neither would he stop Drake in attempting to gather more information on who they were and who they worked for.

After calling Drake, Rachel rang the head waiter in the dining room and told Charlene to place the out of breath "boys" closer to the middle of the room.

Charlene did as she was told as the two goons were laughing out loud creating a stir amongst the other diners.

No matter, Rachel thought, as she handed two spike drinks to Charlene to take to their table. "Compliments of the Hotel", she told Charlene.

Rachel knew that the drinks would buy Drake some additional time in his discovery who the guys were.

Using a master key from Rachel, Drake was able to enter the room unnoticed. The two beds were a little rumpled as they appeared to be where they were sitting on them. Their clothes however were neatly hung in the closet and the four drawers were separated for each man, with underwear, socks, sweaters, and shirts precisely placed.

After sipping their water and drinks, their salads arrived and Giuseppe asked Juan for the paperwork from their boss in Tampa to go over.

Beginning to feel the drink, Juan was smiling a little and said, "No, I don't have them, I thought you had them?"

Giuseppe slightly laughing, made a feeble attempt at looking for them padding his outside pockets then excused himself, stood up and started towards the elevator.

Rachel noticing Giuseppe's departure, from the dining room stopped him as he approached to leave and asked. "Is everything alright?"

"Yes", smiling Giuseppe, "I musta forgot something in my room and need to find it before it is lost. A stupid mistake but not to worry, Giuseppe is always on the job!"

"Oh, alright", Rachel replied, as he strolled to the elevator.

Watching him walk, Rachel noticed that the drink was taking effect on him by his clumsiness.

By now, Giuseppe was sweating profusely, but laughing at himself, because he knew what it would mean if he lost the papers entrusted to them by Tampa.

Reaching inside his jacket to grab his handkerchief he touched the fabric of the hankie and luckily felt the papers and stopped before getting onto the elevator.

Smiling and laughing out loud boisterously, he turned back around and proceeded to the table where Juan was laughing too for some unknown reason, as Giuseppe sat down.

"Everything Okay" Juan asked.

"Yep", said Giuseppe. "Thought I'd left those damn papers in the room, but alas my friend, I have them in my pocket. How else would we know what to do next!"

For Drake the room netted almost nothing until he saw the small writing tablet on the desk by the phone. It read, "Danny and Ashley, need to be eliminated. Take your time and do what is necessary without any trail".

Curious why they would leave such a note laying around, it also told him that they were careless and probably simple and might make other mistakes that would help the police.

Drake wondered who they might be talking to that would hold that much power over them to direct them to write such a thing down. It was certainly self-incrimination…

Looking around the room one more time, Drake made sure before leaving that nothing was out of place. Finished, he closed the door and started walking down the hall as the two goons stepped out of the elevator, very drunk, bumping into each other and laughing as they approached Drake and said to him, "Buona notte Senior, Arrivederci!".

Drake smiled back at them and then turned the corner and stopped. He quickly glanced around the edge of the wall to see what they were doing. There was a lot of noise as Juan was on his hands and knees looking for the key to the room. Giuseppe was going through each pocket to see if he had it and by accident the instruction documents that were inside his jacket fell out onto the floor as Juan stood up holding the key and smiling at Giuseppe.

Laughter continued to fill the hall as they keyed the door and let themselves in, leaving the papers in the hallway.

Drake couldn't believe his luck and ran down the hall as quiet and quickly as he could grabbing the documents before heading for the stairs. Without stopping, he ran down to the lobby, now out of breath, as Rachel walked up to him smiling.

"How was your run, DB, a little late don't you think?", she murmured to him.

"Great. Thank you again. I owe you big time", said Drake.

"You can count on it" replied Rachel.

Saratoga Springs
Chapter 8

After saying goodnight to Rachel, Drake walked to the
concierge desk and asked to use the phone and called the
Police Chief. That night at the station Sam and Drake
looked through the papers thoroughly.

Sam wasn't surprised to find out who was behind the hit on
the couple. It all added up since Allen and Doris knew
where the money came from originally to establish
themselves in the town. It was only fitting that the
Syndicate wanted to keep things tidy without
boomeranging back to them.

Drake was amazed that they would be so brazen to do such
a thing in this day and age. But then he had been out of the
picture for a while and apparently, the new days were not
so different than the old days when it came to money and
the Syndicate.

There was an explicit note to the two men telling them to
round up Danny and Ashley and wait for further
instructions. They were to use the Stein boat to keep them
safe and handy. Additional instructions would be given to
the two men on what to do next. However, Danny and
Ashley's demise needed to look normal, or as normal as
possible. Danny who thought of himself as an "up and
coming big-shot" within the Family, didn't think that
anything could happen to him.

It was signed only with initials, "SA".

Neither Sam nor Drake knew who this could be but
knowing that the guys came from the Tampa area, they had

their hunch that the men were connected to the Family there.

Sam took the papers and asked one of the police officers to make copies using the latest department purchase of a Xerox machine. When the officer was done, he returned them to Sam, who then handed them back to Drake.

Returning to the hotel, DB had replaced the papers just as he found them, in the exact envelop. Walking up to the front desk, he turned them into lost and found, as Giuseppe's name was on the outside of the envelop.

He then told the concierge to leave a message for the guys informing them that there was an envelope for them at the front desk.

When the two hung over guys awoke the next morning, it took them almost two hours to get themselves ready. It was nearly nine thirty when Giuseppe noticed that the lining of his inside jacket pocket had been turned outside and there were no papers.

Panicked, he started shouting and cursing at Juan who had just stepped out of the bathroom whistling.

"You stupida cagna, why did you drink so much, we lost the papers and will no doubt lose our heads over this. What the hell are we going to do. We can't tell anyone about this, otherwise we will be visited by some others shortly. What are we going to do, Christ I am stupida too!"

Sitting by the phone Juan was about to tie his shoes when he noticed the light blinking. He waved his arms at Giuseppe to tell him "be quiet" as he placed the phone to his ear. Then as Giuseppe mumbled something under his breathe, Juan said, "Hello, yes this is room 436, is there a message for us?"

"Yes, came the response. Someone found an envelope that belongs to Mr. D'Angelo and placed it with us. You can pick it up when you are down stairs."

"Fabuloso, mucho aprecio", replied Juan as Giuseppe yelled, "Speak English!"

"Oh, so sorry Sir", Juan then said. "Yes, yes, we will pick it up when we come down for breakfast."

Hanging up the phone, Juan smiled and whispered, "Well Senior Giuseppe, we get to keep our heads a little bit longer. The envelope was found on the floor in the hotel and someone turned it in."

Laughing and jumping up and down, as if he just won the lottery Juan waved his arms in the air at Giuseppe, who was not amused at all.

"We better be careful from here on in", Giuseppe remarked. "This is serious and we shouldn't be taking it so lightly."

"True", quipped, Juan "Let's go!"

Saratoga Springs
Chapter 9

Over many decades, Saratoga Springs was the location for
the national meeting of the Mafia, with members attending
from near and far. Chicago of course, Los Angeles, Miami,
Tampa, Cleveland, New York and Boston.

It was held once a year religiously with very few occasions
of being interrupted by state or federal representatives
trying to close each Family down.

Sometimes the "barbeques" included state, federal and
community members enjoying themselves in the throes of
the gangsters while other times, they stood side by side
with the police and the FBI agents, as they rounded them
up.

Occasionally, members of each family would go on a
vacation after such an assault, in order to "lay low" until
the incident blew over from being on the front-page news.

Though Allen and Doris were investigated several times,
they were never carted off to jail.

Allen was as shrewd as his father, Hiram, who worked for
the "Family" as an associate. Even though Miami was the
major partner in the Tampa enterprise, "Hy", as they called
him. was able to save money for his son to help in the
establishment of the "clothing business". This appeared
legit to anyone on the outside, but in fact was funded
primarily from the bootlegging and gambling monies
received into the "Family" and used for the same in the
replenishing of those funds.

Hy passed away from natural causes shortly after the clothing store opened for business. So he never saw the rewards that his son and grandson enjoyed.

Daybreak came with Danny on the boat getting unruly. He felt that he did his job for Sonny, as requested. who Danny thought was in control of the situation. He believed that being stuck on the boat with Ashley was unreasonable in regard to what he did and what Ashley knew. Just because she saw names of members on a document did not implicate them in destroying the buildings by fires and then building new ones to take over control of the property.

Danny felt that she was too young to truly understand what was happening. So he wanted off the boat and called his Dad to see what he could do.

Following the conversation with his son, Allen drove to the hotel to find Giuseppe and Juan to see what could be done. Finding them having breakfast, he walked over and asked, "May I sit down?"

Juan replied, "Si, have a seat, what can we do for you?"

Allen explained that his son was getting stir-crazy and wanted to know when he could get off the boat.

Giuseppe was first to speak and said, "Mr. Stein, as instructed by you know who, your son is to remain on the boat along with the girl till we are told otherwise. Though, if you wish to contact Tampa, in the meantime, by all means. But do so quickly and have them contact us with their final decision. You do understand, yes?"

Allen shook his head and replied, "Yes, I will contact them shortly and I am sure they will let you know the outcome. Thank you for your time."

Noticing the exchange at their table, Rachel saw Allen leave the hotel, while the goons chuckled.

Rachel then went to the front desk and called Drake. Fortunately, she was able to reach him as he was just putting on his coat to leave.

"Late night" she asked.

"Oh yes", replied Drake. "Not much fun if you know what I mean, but I did have a good time…"

"Well listen", as Rachel told Drake about Allen and the two goons.

Drake responding said, "Before this is over, I will owe you more than I think I can afford!"

Rachel chuckled and replied, "I am sure than you can work it off for me. It's been a long time, if you know what I mean."

This time, Drake laughed out loud and said, "For me too, so yes, when this is all over."

"Thanks again. I will catch up with you later."

"Okay", Rachel replied and hung up the phone.

As he drove to his store Allen wondered what SA would say. After walking into the haberdashery, Allen looked at his wife Doris, who asked, "Well how did it go?"

"It didn't", replied Allen. "I've got to call SA and try to arrange something else. This is gotten out of hand. I just wanted to scare our son and that Ashley girl. They have taken it to a whole other level."

Doris, started to weep, when Allen told her to leave so he could contact Tampa and try to work out a reasonable solution.

Saratoga Springs
Chapter 10

In the scheme of things, the incident and problems in
Saratoga was nothing compared to other larger issues
hampering the Tampa Family and their "investments".

One such situation involved a member who was a rancher
in the upcoming Pasco County area, muscling in on other
ranchers and taking over property upon property to grow
the farming business for the Syndicate.

Though the Feds were onto the man, he was unaware that
he was being targeted and wiretapped. After being
arrested, it put a damper on control of farming for the
Tampa gang, so they moved their operations towards Plant
City.

Still in Hillsborough County, Plant City held a different set
of problems. Latinos and blacks worked the fields and
many Southern farmers would break out their rifles on what
many saw as Tampa Cubanos trying to cut into their land or
profits.

Cotton fields had turned into cattle farming and strawberry
fields that yielded incredible cash for anyone willing to
work the land. Hence SA and his operation wanted in or
wanted to control as much as he could. For a while he was
able to muster up enough power to get his piece of the pie,
but even that began to erode away because the Feds were
now looking at the drugs being poured into the small town
along with gambling and prostitution, after so many of the
local southern Baptist farmers complained.

As legend has it, the hanging of a couple of farmers didn't
scare off the others and soon SA had to pull out of the area

tucking his tail between his legs as he was chased back to Ybor City.

No one knows for sure if the Feds had started the legend or if it came via Giuseppe and Juan who were the muscle in town.

The additional chaos in Saratoga was based around the larger stake in the racetrack business. Sonny and Moe were constantly at each other's throat over the major issue of paying money to the Allen who divided it up into the Families across the States. Each of them felt that the fees that were being extracted were too extravagant for their businesses and that the Allen and Doris were making money without having to pay their fair share.

When the conversation amongst some of the Families evolved, it was determined that Allen's son Danny and the Fire Chief's daughter, Ashley, both needed to go away permanently. Allen strongly disagreed and said that he was willing to pay more to Tampa in order to keep his son alive. But SA, had made his decision and Allen accepted it and later told his wife who wept for hours.

After the two goons in Saratoga got the final decision from SA, they figured that the best way to get rid of the two would be on the boat.

Planning out the destruction of the yacht and demise the young couple would take a little time. Giuseppe told Juan that they would need several cans of regular gasoline for the yacht, and a small boat with engine that was not registered. This way it couldn't be traced back to them. Furthermore, they would need to purchase their plane tickets for an early morning flight to Tampa, so they would not be suspected.

Juan set about driving through town, looking for gasoline containers when he happened by one of two gas stations in town.

There was an old man running the station when he pulled up in his limo and had to wake him up to purchase gas. Juan asked him, "What time do you open and close?"

The old man replied, "I am usually here by 8 every morning and close right before 10 at night. Say you are not from around here, are you?"

Juan smiled a devilish grin and said, "No Senior, I am from Tampa, but I am up here on business for my boss. Muy apreciado for the information, in case I need some gas on my trip."

The old man looked at Juan curiously but said nothing and went back into the garage where he went back to sleep.

Two nights later, Juan crept into the back door, which was unlocked and found two empty gas cans. As he was about to leave, he heard someone opening up the front door. It was the old man. He was mumbling to himself as he went to the cash register and opened it up and took out a twenty dollar bill, closed the drawer and started walking towards the front door when he heard a metal tinkling sound.

The old man turned and yelled out, "Who goes there? Whoever you are, you better leave before I call the cops!"

Juan froze not knowing what to do, creating such a silence that he could hear his own heart beating like something from "Marcus Welby MD". He swear that the old man could hear it too, but then the old man mumbled again and said, "Damn rats!" and walked out the door and locked it behind him.

Sweat was pouring down Juan's face. His shirt was stuck to his chest. He leapt to the back door, cans banging against whatever was on each side of him and as he reached for the handle, the door swung open onto his foot, causing him to winch as the old man opened with a large flashlight in his hand. Blinded by the light, Juan rushed past him into the pitch black of the night knocking him over and out.

By the time Juan got back to the room, he was soaked, but laughed about the story as he told Giuseppe, though his foot hurt like hell.

When the cops took down the statement from the old man, he was still talking it up.

He said, "If I had known that there was someone in my garage, I would have taken a tire iron and cracked that kid in the head."

"How'd you know it was a kid." The police officer taking the statement asked.

"Who else would be in the garage at night. Never got a clean look at him. Probably looking for something to steal and sell. You know how kids are. Besides, I didn't find any of my tools missing and it didn't feel like an adult as he ran passed me, but then it could have been a girl for all I know, it was dark and my eyes aren't what they used to be..."

When Sam got the report, he filed it away not thinking too much about the incident. It seemed innocent enough from what the old man said. So Sam thought no more about it.

A few days later, as dusk was settling, to be sure that Juan hadn't been recognized, he and Giuseppe drove to the station to fill up the cans. They had decided that they would pretend to gas up the limo and get the old man to walk back into the office where the cash register was located for change.

Giuseppe's job would be to go with the old man, while Juan filled up the cans that were in the back seat.

So after driving up to the pumps, the old man came out of the station and walked up to Juan and asked, "How can I help you?"

Wearing a hat this time, Juan replied, to make sure that he was not recognize, "Can you fill it up?"

"Sure" replied the old man. But as he was about to pump the gas, Giuseppe spoke up. "Scusi, may I bother you for some change. I have a twenty but need to break it into a couple of fives and a ten. Can you help me out?"

"Yes sir", the old man replied, "But don't you want to wait to see how much your bill will be?"

"No, no Senior", replied Giuseppe, my friend here is paying for the gas today. I only need some change as I owe him $5.00."

"OK, the old man said, then turned towards Juan and asked,

"Is it Ok young feller that I take care of this first?"

"Si Si" replied, a smiling Juan.

As Giuseppe and the old man walked towards the office, Juan opened the back door and proceeded to take out the two cans and fill them up before they returned.

After returning the cans to the floor of the back seats, he shut door, then placed the nozzle into the limo's gas tank and began pumping it as the old man and Giuseppe came back around to the car.

"Oh, said the old man, I am sorry I didn't mean for you to pump your own gas?"

"It's Ok", said Juan "I am done, just trying to help out."

"Well, that's pretty nice of you, young feller."

Then the old man looked at the meter and said to him, "Wow that car sure eats up a lot of gas. That'll be $15.43!"

After paying the bill, the limo sped away and the old man went back in the garage thinking to himself, "Didn't I meet that Spanish guy before?"

Saratoga Springs
Chapter 11

When both Sonny and Moe found out the decision
regarding Danny and Ashley, from SA, they immediately
called him to object to his verdict. They felt that any
unnecessary attention like this would only fall back on
them hard. The politicians and locals would point their
fingers at them since most everyone knew who they were
and where the money came from and went.

SA was not concerned. He told both racetrack owners the
kids were a nuisance and to resolve their own difference or
else.

After calling Miami, Moe and Sonny felt a bit more at ease
that it could be handled in another manner and that there
would be more conversations with Tampa before anything
else would happen. Thoughtlessly, the two goons were
going about their business as originally planned and hadn't
heard about Miami's decision.

Babysitting the couple on the yacht were BS jobs according
to Juan and Giuseppe. The guys wanted to get back to
some sunshine and out of the winter doldrums. However
they also knew that it was their job to complete it without
complaining about it or leaving a trace to them or anyone
else.

Giuseppe was having a hard time finding a small dingy
with an engine, when he located one in a winter storage
shed. It was listed in the local paper that indicated that it
was for sale since the original owner had vacated the
property and left it behind.

The storage shed, was close to the neighborhood of Harbor Bay and Point Breeze Marina.

After visiting the location without actually going into the facility, Giuseppe planned to steal the dingy at night. All they had to do was find a truck with a tow bar to transport the boat to a secret spot in a cove.

Asking around, Giuseppe was able to locate a towing yard service that was on the edge of town. When Giuseppe and Juan drove by, they noticed a name they were familiar with, DiCarlo.

Returning to their hotel room, they called a number all too acquainted with Tampa and asked if there was a connection to Manny DiCarlo in Tampa, which was part of the SA gang. It was. So Tampa arranged for a tow truck to be repainted in a neutral color with no markings on it so Giuseppe and Juan could tow the dingy out of the yard.

A few nights later, the two goons drove their limo to the tow yard then jumped into the unmarked tow truck with fake paper plates as if just purchased.

Proceeding to the storage shed they passed the night cop at State Road 9 on their way to Saratoga Lake.

The cop was eating a hoagie from Roma Foods and noticed the strange looking tan truck drive by, but neither called it in or followed it.

Arriving at the yard, they found it locked so Giuseppe got out of the truck and went searching in the back for something to break the chain. Meanwhile Juan jumped out and ran to the fence, took out his never used lock picks and

54

began to fiddle with the two picks in hopes of opening the device.

Watching Juan try to open up the lock, he yelled in his broken English, "Moveda aside. Let il experto takea care of dis!"

Just as Giuseppe was about to cut the lock with the chain cutter, somehow Juan's luck miraculously popped the lock using his metal picks.

Giuseppe was so impressed with his partner, they both smiled at each other and started to laugh out loud.

Juan then got off his knees and swung the gate wide open as Giuseppe ran back to the truck and drove into the shed and over to the boat on the trailer.

The guys hitched it up and drove back out the gate, where Juan re-locked the device as if nothing had occurred.

Driving down to the cove without being noticed the two goons were carrying on so much they almost ran off the road.

However, after leaving the marina and around a small forested area, they found a cove with an old wooden bridge that appeared to be from the forgotten and decrepit bunkhouse 500 feet from the shore. Next to the bridge was a clamp of trees where the two guys were able to place the boat, hiding it from anyone on the shore.

Satisfied with themselves and the covert operation of the night they drove back to their limo at the tow yard, but not before the cop who had seen them before, noticed the neutral color truck again and took down the fake paper license plate number. He was going to check it out because he hadn't seen this truck before in town.

The cop then decided to follow them but made sure that he was far enough behind that he would not be seen.

When the limo stopped after driving out through the gate a guy with a hat got out of the car and locked the gate, then the limo drove away. Everything seemed normal to the cop as he waited to see the tan truck reappear.

Meanwhile the goons were laughing up a storm, driving back to the hotel.

After about an hour or so, the cop realized that he'd been had and that whoever was driving the limo were the same guys in the truck. Realizing it was way too late to go chasing a limo at that time of night, he decided to go back to his post and make a report when he returned to the station.

The goons on the return to town decided to visit the only Saratoga casino in town and try their hands at blackjack.

This "real" club was still in existence even after years of backroom poker tables, and though not owned by the Family it paid large sums for the protection of the premises that were laundered through the Stein stores.

Ironically, even if the goons lost their money, they would be reimbursed by someone within the Family. That night they basically broke even so no one was any of the wiser about who they were.

The next morning there was a report from the owner at the storage shed indicating that someone had stolen a dingy that was for sale. The problem was that it looked like an inside job since the lock had not been cut, so the police placed the report in the "Pending" basket.

Strangely, when the night cop arrived for his shift the following evening, he tried to run a registration report on the numbers he had written down. Befuddled, he determined that the numbers were fake and told the Lieutenant who then informed Sam.

The Police Chief looked at it curiously since this was the third incident in just a few days that seemed very strange for a town so quiet.

That evening over dinner with Drake, Sam brought up the incidents and Drake's ears seem to perk up and asked Sam, "Do you suppose our two out-of-towner foreigners are up to something no good. It sure looks like it to me!"

"Could be" replied Sam. "Nothing much has changed on the yacht situation though there appears to be food delivered there on a daily basis and the two goons have gone there every day sometimes twice."

"Perhaps we need to tail them as well, as we haven't heard anything else, except that Allen and Doris have been absent from their stores. This is a bit strange too. Maybe we should knock on their door to see if they know anything. At least it might rattle the chains, so to speak."

Sam agreed and decided that the following morning they would visit the Stein house once more. He also planned to place two officers on duty to follow the two Tampa guys.

Saratoga Springs
Chapter 12

In discussing their dilemma the Allen decided to try and help their son get off the boat and hide him till the whole thing blew over. However, they didn't know what to do with the girl. Doris thought they should just drop her off at the Williams home unharmed of course, but Allen wasn't so sure.

First, they would have to get to the yacht and get them off the boat without being seen. Plus, they would no doubt have to answer to SA in case he accused them of some sort of sabotage.

It was enough to cause a nervous breakdown. Who could they trust and use without employing anyone from the Families in Chicago, Tampa and Miami? Who was left?

Deciding to ask an old standby who lived in the Tampa area, and only played by his rules, Allen was able to reach out to Alphonso Francisco. Alphonso was known to sometimes cross both sides of the street during any involvement or disagreement.

Alphonso, who was known as "Nunso", was a hired gun by all Families including those in Italy. He had also turned on some family members in the past, so that he wouldn't have to pull the trigger. A shrewd but quiet player, most bosses never turned their back on him for fear that he would kill a relative or themselves. Even the Feds were a bit scared of him. He was like a shadow that disappeared without a trace.

Nunso happened to be Danny's godfather, so it was only right that he be asked to assist in the kid's safety.

At first Nunso said, "no". but after listening to the whole story from Doris and then from Allen he agreed to help him vanish, but only if Nunso could decide where to send him and for how long.

With their approval, Allen gave Nunso the time table that he thought the two goons were working on.

Nunso agreed to place his current responsibilities on hold and fly up the following morning.

Disliked by both of the guys from Tampa, Nunso had tread on some of their territory before and seemed to come out of it smelling like a rose while Giuseppe and Juan almost had to beg for their lives. Hence there was no great love between the three hoodlums.

When Sam and Drake drove to the Stein gate the next morning, the guard recognized Sam immediately and smiled as he stopped to chit chat.

The guard was a retired beat cop from New York City, but knew Sam from all the police benefits held in Saratoga cops, which he attended.

As they drove up the rough stone driveway, Drake was totally taken back by the size of the property and the amount of hired help that would be needed to care for it.

Drake said to Sam, "Christ, they must be laundering an incredible amount of money for the Syndicate. There is no way that a clothing store could be making that much money from suits and shirts."

"Sam snickered and replied, "Well not everyone buys their duds from the Salvation Army or some other thrift shop!

Besides who said that either Stein shop is only for buying clothes? There's off track betting, back room poker and of course the lake casinos, that they have their fingers in. Though my only deduction is because no one has ever told me anything different. But like you, I know that they couldn't afford such a place without some other help, legal or otherwise!"

Drake replied, "I knew it!"

After walking up the steps to the house, as Sam was about to knock on the door, it opened with the butler standing to the side inviting them in.

Drake looked at Sam, but they both knew that the guard at the gate had rung up the main house to tell them that they were driving up.

The butler was polite enough asking them to join him in the parlor and await Mr. Stein.

Inside the room's dark oak walls, they were covered in photographs and etchings of horses except in the center of the room, where a very large painted picture of the three Steins over-shadowed everything else.

Curiously, Bill Williams stable logo was part of the painted background which Drake and Sam hadn't realized until that very moment that he might be involved.

Drake was not amused, and Sam was upset for not thinking that Bill might have some involvement.

Drake looking back at Sam said, "Are you kidding?"

Just then Allen Stein opened the two doors and entered the parlor stating, "I am sorry for the short delay. Trying to get this sharkskin design from Italy and it's taking too long and I've got Mr. Rockefeller on my back for delivery of his suits in one week. Anyway, that's my trouble, how may I help you?"

Sam looked at Allen with a "huh" glance. He was a bit shocked that Allen's own son had disappeared and that it seemed to matter not. Drake too was also puzzled, since they knew why Sam was there but didn't know who Drake was or remembered him in his current attire, grey beard, tan face and long hair. Mr. Stein never even asked who Drake was? It was mind boggling to say the least to both of the detectives.

Looking at Sam, then Drake, Stein took another posture, "I am sorry, I know why you are here. It's my son. Yes, we are concerned to about his disappearance, but he's done this before so we are not to too concern. You know how young men can be, right?"

Sam, the ever polite policeman, got to the point. "Mr. Stein not only are we concerned about Danny's whereabouts but we are concerned about the incident in which he shoved Ashley Williams into his car and neither of them have been seen since."

Drake could see beads of perspiration beginning to form on Allen's forehead.

Allen was about to say something but was cut off by Sam.

"Mr. Stein, we also know that there are two members from an Italian family that reside in Tampa who have been seen with you during the last week or so. This bothers me in that all I can think about is that these two guys are somehow involved with the kids' disappearance and that this leads to you and to Tampa alike. Am I making myself clear to you Allen?"

Stein was now drenched with streams of sweat rolling down his cheeks.

Allen tried to calm down and replied, "Sam, we go back a long time. I've asked for some help in locating Danny and Ashley. This is why they are here, nothing more. We know that you are doing the best that you can do, but I thought that if I could help that would be a plus for everyone, okay? I am still mystified by my son's actions and want to get to the bottom of it."

Sam wasn't buying his reasoning, nor was Drake.

Just as Sam was about to say something, Doris walked in, or as Drake told Sam later, "waddled in", all 280 pounds of her. She was breathing heavy as she strode across to where Allen was standing.

Next to Allen, who may have been 160 pounds soaking wet, they looked like cartoon characters, as Drake wondered, "how in the hell..." Now he understood why Bill went out on medical retirement.

Doris thought she murmured her statement to Allen, but in fact Drake heard it loud and clear, since he was standing closer to her than Sam.

She said, "Mr. Nunso has arrived and is anxious to get busy with his task."

Allen snapped his head towards Doris and said, "Okay, I'll be there in a moment. I need to finish up with the Chief first!"

Doris, who was oblivious to what she had said and what was happening in the parlor, turned herself around and trotted back out.

Allen apologized for his wife's interruption, then said, "Sam if I can do anything else or shed some more information on Danny or Ashley's disappearance, I will call you immediately. Okay?"

Sam knew he wouldn't hear anything back but said, "Alright".

Then Drake and Sam were ushered out of the room by Allen and said, "Thank you."

In the car as they drove back to the station, Drake told Sam what he heard from Doris, then asked "Could this be the same guy that Miami used in New York over the bootlegging scam?"

Sam smiled and said, "No doubt. We need to find out where he is and put a tail on him. It's getting a little too thick with thieves here in our charming town."

Saratoga Springs
Chapter 13

As soon as Sam and Drake left, Allen ran out of the house
and drove to the Adelphi to pick up Nunso.

No one was the wiser or knew about the dapper man, as the
front desk clerk assigned Mr. Francisco's room innocently,
next to Drake on the second floor.

After checking in, he was taken to his room but appeared
back in the lobby in a very short time.

"Dressed to the nines", said Rachel to Drake later. "He
was somewhat dashing looking, like an older Clark Gable,
with black shinny hair and deep black eyes and a pencil
moustache."

Rachel then told Drake that Allen had picked him up and
they left in a hurry.

Drake concerned that they might have missed their chance
in following him, immediately called Sam to relay what
had taken place.

Sam then told two plain clothes cops who were at their
desks to use an unmarked car and drive to the Stein house
and follow Allen and the Italian man that was with him.

In the meantime, Drake asked Rachel's help once again.

Drake needed to look in Nunso's room, so he obtained a
master key and walked next door to see if he could find out
why and what he was there for.

Just like the two goons, very little was laying about to indicate what his plans were, so Drake left the room appearing untouched and returned the key to Rachel.

Sitting in her office, Drake was pondering his thoughts about Nunso when Rachel asked him, "Do you want my people to keep tabs on Mr. Francisco?"

"Yes, that would be great", Drake replied. "We have to figure out what his instructions are from Allen and the timetable that he is working on."

"Alright", smiled Rachel, "But that 'I Owe You' that you owe Me is getting larger every day."

Drake leaned over to Rachel, kissed her on the cheek and said, "I'll be ready when you are!"

Driving to the marina, Allen explained the whole scenario and situation to Nunso. However, he wasn't interested in who, what or where, just his job. In other words, "What did Allen want him to do? Nothing more, nothing less!"

Allen saw that all the details he was telling Nunso were just annoying him, so he decided to just tell him what he wanted done.

"Listen", Allen said, "I need for you to extract the boy and girl on the boat. However, how you do it is up to you. I do not have any problems with that. Nor do I care about the two idiots up here from Tampa. If you need to, drop the girl off at my home or hotel and I will take it from there. As for my son, you will make the determination where to send him and I am Ok with that."

Nunso just nodded his head and said, "Let's take a look at where the yacht is, so I get my bearings."

Pulling up to Dalvi Aquatic Boat Rentals, in Manning's Cove, Angelo Dalvi was waiting for them, as Allen had called him to tell him that they would need his assistance.

After a few words, Angelo got into the twin engine Crowne 250 and started the engines with a roar as Allen and Nunso stepped aboard.

Moments later they were about half way to the yacht, around three quarters of a mile parallel to the shoreline. The lake was not large by any means from shoreline to shoreline, except the length of the lake was almost five miles long, while the width was only about 1 and a half miles.

As instructed Angelo slowed the boat down as Nunso took the binoculars out of the case and looked up and down the lake and from shoreline to shoreline taking in the size of the yacht and how he might climb aboard it in the night. Satisfied with his findings he told Allen that he was done and they could return to the dock.

But just as they were starting their way back, Danny had come outside, on deck and tried waving to the Crowne.

Nunso, who saw this ignored him, since he didn't want to take any chance during daylight of rescuing the couple.

Back at the marina, Nunso told Allen and Angelo to just leave the keys under the seat and to make sure that he could get into Manning's Cove sometime after 11PM that night.

After it was all set up, Allen drove Nunso back to the hotel.

Nunso wanting it to be clear with Allen said, "When this is completed, I expect payment in full and I will tell you where your son is. As far as the girl is concerned, I will bring her to you so you can deal with the aftermath. It is not my concern."

Allen shook his head in agreement.

Saratoga Springs
Chapter 14

Unaware that Nunso was in town and two floors beneath them, the two Tampa boys received the phone call they were waiting for from SA and decided that on Monday night they would take care of the situation. It was Saturday afternoon and the only thing to do was to watch basketball and of course "bet on the ponies", eat and wait another day and a half.

Sitting at the desk, Giuseppe asked Juan, "Morning, afternoon or evening flight?"

Juan smiling said, "Let's get out of town first thing in the morning. I don't want to be hanging around when the cops start snooping and asking everyone questions."

"Right" replied Giuseppe. "Besides, I'm tired of the cold weather and need my sunshine."

After setting up the flights, Giuseppe called down for room service and they settled in to watch TV.

Rachel was in the kitchen speaking with the main chef and heard the order being written down. She went over to Carlos when he hung the phone and looked at the order.

"Is everything alright, Ms. Rachel?"

"Oh yes Carlos, just looking at what they ordered. Thanks."

Next, Rachel called Drake's room to see if he was there. He was not. So she called Sam at the station to see if he was there and to tell him what the two guys were doing.

He was not there neither, but Sam told Rachel that he would give Drake the message if he saw him first.

That afternoon, Drake was burning up the rubber driving around the lake to better understand the situation and possible recourse.

He noticed that the yacht had been moved out to a mooring spot almost in the center of the lake.

Drake now believed that it was one way to keep someone captive or hidden without any visitors snooping around.

In the cool air of the afternoon, he made his way from one side to the other stopping at various points to look around to see if anything was peculiar.

As Drake slowly drove beyond the docks and then to the Harbor Bay marina, he made his way just past a small wooden area of cypress trees. Something shiny in the afternoon light caught his eyes as he was scanning the waterfront. He stopped the car and walked down the bank to get a better look and found the missing trailer with the dingy tied to it already in the water, waiting to be used.

Getting back in the car Drake made a mental note to tell Sam about the dingy as he drove around to the other side where he ended up at the Manning's Cove Boat Marina. Since no one knew who he was, he thought he'd asked some questions about boat rentals.

The first guy he met, was repairing a hole in the bottom of a twenty five foot Crowne. It looked like it had run aground by the size of the hole. But the kid didn't know what the costs would be or if any were still available. He suggested that Drake go to the office where someone would be able to help.

Peering down the docks, Drake saw a Crowne that appeared to have just been used, since another boat helper was wiping it down.

Walking into the office Drake asked about the Crowne, when the guy behind the counter said, "It's not for rent. It's already spoken for by Mr. Francisco. He's supposed to use it today or tomorrow, I think. Anyway it belongs to the owner and he lent it to that guy from Tampa."

"Okay" said Drake and left the office, smiling to himself. He knew just by being casual, he'd gotten more information out of the counter guy than the counter guy was supposed to share.

Nonetheless, he needed to get back to the station and brief Sam so they could figure out their next move.

Saratoga Springs
Chapter 15

Sam and Drake huddled in Police Chief's office, for fear that anything they said would get out before it was supposed to or to anyone with knowledge of Danny or Ashley whereabouts.

With apparently two different situations involving the couple on the boat, neither the Police Chief nor Drake were unsure of what direction they should take.

The two goons from Tampa apparently wanted to kill the two kids while it was unsure of what Nunso was going to do, particularly since he was hired by Allen.

In the end it was agreed that Sam would round up the Tampa two, and Drake would discover and prohibit Nunso from completing his task while in the Springs.

Meanwhile the phone was ringing off the hook at the Stein Mansion. Danny threatened to jump off the boat and swim to the banks of the lake. But Allen convinced him to wait, that he had a plan and that both he and Ashley would be safe. "Besides" as Allen told Danny, "If you jump into the lake, you'll never make it to shore with the lake water being a frozen 28 degrees."

Danny agreed to sit tight for the moment while his Dad figured a way to get him off the boat and into a safe place.

By this time Ashley was going stir-crazy herself by not having any contact with anyone, other than her captors. Danny wouldn't allow her to use the phone and insisted that she stay in her stateroom. Though she threatened and cussed him, he locked her up each day, telling her that it was for her own good. Except for food and the daily five minutes topside, she was locked up per instructions from the two goons. Danny thought that he was safe and didn't know that he was a target as well.

Feeling like he was of importance, sometimes Danny would be able to get ahold of Juan or Giuseppe in their hotel room, by phone, but not often enough, so this drove him crazy. But when he did reach them, they told him some baloney story to keep him in check.

On Sunday at the spa resort, Roosevelt Baths, which was established in 1935 thanks to President Franklin Roosevelt, the two from Tampa, after breakfast, drove over to soak in the hydrotherapy waters.

Unaware that an unmarked police car had followed them that day and would stick close by to keep tabs on them.

In their Jeep, making good time, on this particular damp Sunday, Sam and Drake were able to find the Ninth District Coast Guard Auxiliary Commodore, Mike Brown to speak with him about a potential problem. They drove to the dock where the Guard kept their boats. It was located on Fish Creek, which extended all the way to the Hudson River. Some parts of the "Creek" were very small and other passages had waterfalls and rapids.

Fish Creek was famous during the bootlegging days of prohibition when the whiskey distillery in Canada would float down barges from Hudson Bay to Fish Creek and walk the boats in the creek eventually getting into the Lake. It was a perilous journey but profitable for many along the route, including out of work men, organized crime and the distillery as well.

The Commodore was all too willing to help Sam and Drake, since he knew them from years of playing poker together. After retiring from the Coast Guard, Mike lived in Wilton, a short drive up route 9.

After discussing a plan to seize the Tampa guys and the yacht, the Commodore dispensed one of his boats, with an experienced night Coastie by the nick name of "Brooklyn".

The boat was a Chris Craft 120 HP single engine that originally belonged to the Commodore, who donated it to the Auxiliary. It was the fastest on the lake and very dependable.

Brooklyn told Sam "You tell me when, I will have 'er all set and ready to go."

"Great" said Sam and thanked the Commodore for his help in this matter. Then smiling he said, "I'll see you in a couple of weeks at the card game!" And with that Sam and Drake left.

As decisions were made, Sam told his officers to stay close to the two goons from Tampa, while Drake was to shadow of Nunso. Sam also placed men on duty tailing Allen Stein to make sure that they could control whatever situation was going to occur.

When Sam and Drake returned from Fish Creek, Bill Williams, Ashley's Dad was waiting for them. He was almost in tears, asking them for help in locating his daughter. He kept asking, "Haven't you guys found anything yet?"

Sam said to Bill, "Look we are doing everything we can at the moment. Give us another couple of days. I am sure by then something will have turned up."

"Are you sure Sam? It's been a few weeks now and we still haven't heard anything."

Sam replied, "Bill we are getting closer by the moment for answers, just let us do our jobs and we will notify you as soon as we can."

"All right", said Bill, "But if I don't hear from you then, I will start tearing up this town, if you know what I mean."

After Bill left, Sam turned to Drake and said, "Man he must be going nuts. But I get his gest and I know he will call his old buds at the Fire Department to start digging into this mess. We have got to figure this out and get Ashley back to her Dad as quick as we can."

Drake certainly understood what Sam and Bill were saying. Time was of the essence, but they were waiting on any of the three Tampa guys to make their first moves.

Saratoga Springs
Chapter 16

Monday morning arrived and it was like the rats leaving the building as Nunso left first, with Drake right behind him like a shadow on the wall. Having never met Drake, Nunso was unaware that he was being tailed by the former cop.

Both men had gotten their cars from the hotel valet and drove through town heading to Manning's Cove on a particular grey and chilly February day.

Shortly after Nunso and Drake departed, the two goons came down for their normal breakfast and without noticing the casual plain clothes cop across the room, they ordered their regular platters of eggs, bacon and hash browns.

When they were done, the goons paid their bill and left.

Awaiting the retrieval of their car from the attendant, they the goons wore heavy wool tan coats that made their appearance of out of towner tourists look more like western dusters from the Jesse James gang. The undercover cop however was dressed in an old bomber jacket with a fur collar and smiled at them as they got into their car.

By the time the two guys had gotten to their hidden dingy it was almost noon. Giuseppe was checking the engine and the rest of the equipment while Juan was going through the supplies and their getaway car that he had been able to procure from Mr. Stein after some arm twisting.

The 1968 Lincoln was black like a funeral car with four doors. Everything looked like it was in order for the evening's preparations and escape.

The plain clothes cop that had tailed the goons to the forested area kept well hidden and out of sight but was able to confirm what the two guys were up to. At around 1:30 the limo and the cop were all headed back to the hotel.

The cop then called Sam at the station and told him what he had learned and mentioned that they went back to their room and hadn't left at that point.

Sam thanked the cop and told him that his relief was on the way and everyone would stay in position until the next move by the goons.

In Manning's Cove, Nunso walked directly to the boat and hit the start button. The engine slowly began to come alive as it sputtered once but then roared like a sleeping lion.

Nunso hopped out of the boat, untied the back cleat, then walked up to the front and untied that cleat before jumping back into the boat. He tuned the steering wheel right as the boat started to pull away, heading for the open lake.

Drake had been waiting in his car, and as Nunso left the dock, he got out and walked to the office.

When the guy behind the counter asked, "Can I help you?"

Drake responded, "I need to use your phone if that's ok with you?"

"Sure, it's right here. I'll be in the back room" replied the guy and then walked through the doorway.

Drake watching the boat make its way to the yacht, called the Commodore and told him that Nunso was on his way.

The Commodore, then buzzed the pilot of the small craft waiting at the mouth of the Creek. He was told to stay out of sight but to keep an eye on Nunso and the yacht.

Drake then went back outside to his car where he reached inside and drew out binoculars from the glove compartment and placed them on the bridge of his nose turning the dials ever so slowly.

About a half a mile out he could see Nunso heading straight for the yacht. Drake then looked for the Coastie, and as he searched the shoreline, he found him hiding in the tall grass just left of the mouth of Fish Creek. The morning glare of the sun coming through the clouds, gave away his existence by bouncing off the boat's radar antennae.

Moving the field glasses back towards the yacht, Drake saw Nunso tie up the boat to the ladder alongside the yacht. Nunso then climbed aboard and walked into the cabin.

It seemed like forever, but it was only about thirty minutes had passed before Nunso came out of the cabin followed by Danny and Ashley. There was no drama and it seemed all very normal, which in itself perplexed Drake. He thought they'd be tied up or gagged but it was just three people getting into the Crowne.

Peering through the binoculars, the boat of three pushed off from the yacht and began heading back towards Manning's Cove.

Drake decided that he would call the Commodore to pass on the all clear, so he ran back and asked to use the phone again, before returning to his car, just in time as Nunso's boat pulled in next to the dock.

Sitting in his car, Drake saw that Nunso, Danny and Ashley all casually walked to Nunso's car, got in and drove away.

Drake was more bewildered that it seemed to be too friendly but followed Nunso once again as he crossed through town, unknown where he might be headed.

It was just after 4PM as Nunso's car turned onto Clinton St and drove right up to the Stein Mansion. Drake drove pass the house slowly and stopped at the corner. He then turned the car around and pulled on the other side of the street to keep an eye on what might happen next.

Inside the house, Danny was screaming at his Dad, while Doris had taken Ashley into the parlor to offer her some food and apologies.

Nunso was standing there quietly but then spoke. "Danny, shut up and listen or it will be your last breath."

Danny stopped his antics and looked at Nunso.

Nunso then said, "Being angry with your Father will not resolve anything. It is my job to help in this family squabble that has unfortunately seeped back to the Families. Do you understand what I am saying?"

Danny cocked his head, then said, "I think I do."

Nunso replied, "No I don't think you do. The Families want you dead. You have caused some undo attention here in the Springs, in which additional police efforts have become involved in hunting you down and looking into our businesses."

"But I thought I was doing the right thing?", replied Danny.

"I was doing what Sonny told me to do. It was his suggestion and thought this might help him in his taking over the Racetrack."

Allen was beside himself now, listening to his son. He had gotten himself in deep trouble instigated by Sonny. Allen knew that it would be just a matter of time before it brought down his own family, let alone any dealings in town with the other Families who held interest in the local businesses.

Nunso was not surprised at what he heard, then replied, "Like I said, unfortunately the Families want you dead. Abducting the girl was not a smart idea and if you were going to do that you should have asked someone before taking on that responsibility."

"So what is to be done, then", asked Danny.

Nunso walked up to Allen, looked at Danny and said. "You need to disappear for a while until things cool off. Luckily, I am your god-father, otherwise, I might have been the one to dispose of you. That said, I am taking you to Canada to hole up with some of our associates, where you will work for your freedom to come back to the States. Understand?"

Danny sheepishly looking at his shoes, said, "OK, but what about Ashley?"

Allen then spoke. "She will be returned to her Father unharmed and hopefully Bill will not press charges."

"But", Danny began to say.

"But nothing" Nunso spoke. "She is not your concern, get over it. We have enough issues within the Springs that we don't need any more on our plate."

It was almost 5 PM when Nunso drove his car back onto the street and headed towards the hotel.

Unknown to Drake when he was staking out Stein, and following Nunso back to the hotel, the two guys from Tampa were just getting up from their afternoon nap.

SA had phoned the hotel and spoke to Juan first. "Listen, that hair brain in charge of the Casino was the one who got the kid to abduct the girl. I want his head on a platter. You tell Giuseppe to do the job or I will have his head, got it?"

Juan was sweating, he could feel the heat coming through the phone and motioned to Giuseppe to talk to SA.

As Giuseppe took the phone out of Juan's hand, he stood up from the side of the bed, then sat down only to hear the wrath from SA repeating what he had told Juan.

Now Giuseppe was sweating to. When the phone call was over, the two goons looked at each nervously.

Juan spoke first. "Holy crap, he's pissed. What the hell is wrong with Sonny that he would have crossed the line to take the business from Moe. We might have to postpone our flights tomorrow but I think we need to check out of the hotel in case we need to hide after we burn that yacht tonight."

"But where?" asked Giuseppe.

Juan replied, "At Sonny's. He will help us if he knows that we took the heat off of him or at least he would think that."

"Great idea, brilliant in fact, then we will kill him in his bathtub", chuckled Giuseppe.

Juan smiled like a Cheshire cat, then said, "OK let's get ready to leave and take care of those damn kids!"

Saratoga Springs
Chapter 17

When Nunso got back to the hotel, he missed the two guys
from Tampa by two minutes. They were on the fourth floor
taking the elevator down and Nunso was going up to the
second floor.

Drake who had been taking his time stopped at the desk to
see if Rachel was in. She was, so he meandered behind the
reservations counter to her office, as the two guys walked
up to check out.

The cop who was on duty shadowing the two guys casually
walked over to the counter as they turned to leave, with
their bags. They smiled at the cop as they passed him
walking towards the entrance to their limo.

The cop then checked with the desk clerk about the guys
and was told that they had paid their bill in cash and had
checked out. He then asked to use the phone and called the
station house to relay the news. Sam was there and told the
cop to stay with them and contact him as soon as he saw
what they were up to.

Rachel was her chirpy self, asking Drake what was
happening. He told her what he could and left out some of
the more important police business to keep her and the
hotel safe.

She asked him if he had dinner plans and he told her no.
She then called the kitchen and ordered up breakfast for
two, to be delivered to her suite.

Drake smiled, as he knew where this was going. But he
told her that he needed to know if and when Nunso leaves

the hotel since he was tailing him. She said, "Not to worry tonight, we got your back!"

With that Rachel and Drake walked to her suite on the first floor, leaving behind the daily grind of the hotel business.

Driving through town, Giuseppe and Juan's limo travelled the streets to the secret and protected area where their dingy had been hidden.

The goons did not know as they climbed aboard the small dingy, hidden in the trees that their "couple" had already been rescued. As they pushed away from the shore, they thought that they were almost done and could return to the warmth of Tampa after disposing of all three troublesome individuals requested by SA.

The cop who was tailing the two guys, used his police radio and called Sam to alert him that the dingy had left the shore on its way to the yacht.

Sam thanked the cop and told him to stay put in case they were to head back that way, but he was going to have the Coast Guard pick them up.

Calling the Commodore, Sam gave him the green light, which was then patched through to Brooklyn who was napping on the patrol boat.

The plan was now in motion as Brooklyn fired up the single engine on the Chris Craft and the assistant boatswains' mate went below to pull the rifle, gun and ammo out of the armory.

Using only the night lights the patrol boat eased its way off the shore towards the yacht.

Since there was no moon, only the lights from scattered houses on the shore left shadows and silhouettes of the buoys and the yacht on the water.

The patrol boat could not see the small dingy that the goons were in as they made their way towards the yacht. The dingy had no lights and Juan was gauging where they were from the shoreline and his best guess of where the yacht was tied up in the dark.

With Juan on the front of the dingy, Giuseppe was barking out instructions, "Look right, now left, what do you see?"

Juan was feeling like he was getting whiplash, turning his head right and left and said to Giuseppe, "Shut the fuck up, I can't see anything! Hey, why doesn't Danny have any lights on?"

But just as he said that, there was a loud crack as the dingy ran right into the yacht's stern.

The two guys were startled and sat still, almost deathly silent for a moment hoping that no one onboard or even on the shore heard the noise. Fortunately for them the aluminum frame of the dingy held and there was no damage that they could see in the dark.

Finally, Juan said, "Come on let's do this and the two guys jumped onto the yacht, tying the dingy to the side as they extracted the two cans of gasoline and lighters.

Juan ran to the bow of the ship and started to pour the gasoline over the top of the cabin and both sides of the deck.

Neither guy went below to check on Danny or Ashley. They assumed that the two of them were asleep.

Giuseppe took his can and poured the gasoline around the bridge area and then onto the deck towards the stern, just as Juan had finished. Then throwing the two cans into the bridge area they lit the lighters and flung them onto the deck and the fire took off immediately as the two men rushed back into the dingy, untied it and pushed away.

They waited to pull the engine cord only when they were about 15 feet from the yacht and slowly began to make their way back to the secret spot when all hell broke loose.

The fire on the yacht climbed to about twenty feet in the air and the expulsions came fast and furious as the yacht went up in flames.

Peering through his binoculars Brooklyn could see the small dingy carrying the two men and Giuseppe and Juan now saw the lights coming from the patrol boat and headed back towards the burning yacht to try and hide. They knew that there would not be enough time to get back to their car.

By the time the patrol boat had reached the original spot where they had spotted the two guys, the goons had positioned the dingy in a direct line to reach the other side of the shore.

Meanwhile, the boatswain and Brooklyn tried dousing the yacht initially with water from the patrol boat's firehouse to no avail. It was now becoming a blazing piece of wood, as Brooklyn then drove around the yacht looking for the dingy and found no trace.

Calling the Commodore for instructions, Mike Brown advised Brooklyn to stay out there and continue to look for the two guys.

By the time the goons had gotten to the shore, they were hyperventilating. Yelling at each other, they were trying to figure out what to do next.

Juan said "Let's go on foot. It can't be that far to walk back to the car?"

Giuseppe said, "No, we got to go back by boat, hugging the shoreline, it's the only way!"

Juan finally said, "OK", as they climbed back in and began to putter the dingy towards the mouth of the river, instead of going around past Manning's Cove, thinking that they could make their way this way faster and safely to their car.

Now in almost pitch blackness, except for the shell of the yacht lit up by small red flames, the patrol boat circled it slowly, making an ever wider and wider turn as they looked on all sides of the lake trying to locate the two guys or the dingy.

Just as the patrol boat crossed the bow of what was left of the yacht, a reflection from the mouth of Fish Creek gave the dingy away. The aluminum side had reflected only for a few seconds the two shadows staring straight at the patrol boat.

Brooklyn grab his binoculars and saw that it was the two guys. He then turned on the siren and began to pursue the dingy at high speed.

The goons heard the siren and the roar of the Chris Craft in the still of the night that it was heading their way fast.

Puttering through the mouth and up into the Creek area, it was normally frozen at that time of the year, but the water only had chunks of ice, due to a weak winter of snow.

With the aluminum hull smacking the ice as fast as Giuseppe could make the dingy go, it was a race up the Creek.

Fish Creek is known for its different tributaries. In the spring, summer and fall the cabins along the Creek are filled with families, fishing, rowing or just enjoying themselves relaxing by the waters. There are parts where you have to go on foot, while other parts have rapids.

In a way the goons were fortunate since the Creek was full of water for miles, all the way up to the Lake Erie. But there was an East Branch and a West Branch, where the Erie Canal connected.

Not familiar with the Branches, the guys decided to go into the East Branch which did have rapids but ended as a river about a quarter of a mile up stream, before it reemerged as a treacherous waterway.

Brooklyn was able to almost catch up to the dingy, when Giuseppe made his move hugging the shoreline.

The patrol boat had to reverse quickly before going into the East Branch since it was too shallow and narrow for the craft.

Brooklyn phoned the Commodore to alert him that they couldn't go any further upstream in the patrol boat and they would have to go by foot to follow the two men. But the Commodore told Brooklyn to stay put in case the guys doubled back.

He then phoned the State Police for their help. They told the Commodore that they would try and sandwich them in by having the Police march down from Lake Ave towards the mouth where Brooklyn was standing by.

As Giuseppe and Juan made their way, the State Police were quickly stretching men out at the tiny point where the river came to a dribble, before exploding into the rapids.

Trying to be as quiet as they could be, the Tampa thugs heard the sounds of the police talking and using flashlights to light up the Creek.

Juan motioned to Giuseppe to stop and kill the power of the engine.

Because they were close to the shoreline, they quietly sat and waited as the dingy drifted up against some trees and bushes.

It seemed like hours that they were waiting in the quiet of the night, only listening to the rustle of the wind in the trees and the occasional police officer sneezing or coughing.

As the freezing temperature continued to drop, the guys began to feel the cold air through their dusters as they sat still in the aluminum carcass and the cold water combined magnified the stalemate.

The State Police had become completely died silent turning on a flashlight now and then to shine into the Creek.

Regrettably, it was a standoff, as the Police didn't know that the guys were close to where they were spread out.

An hour and a half had passed. Time seemed to stand still as the two goons bodies began to hurt like hell from just sitting there trying not to make a sound.

Juan had a notebook and pen in his coat and took it out writing down as best as he could in the darkness what he thought they should do.

It read, "Let's leave the damn boat, start walking back on this side until we get to that bridge we went under and cross over and walk back to the car. It's our only chance!"

Giuseppe took the note and held it as close as he could to read it. There was just enough light from a cabin up the road from where they were hiding for him to make out the gibberish that only the two of them understood.

He nodded his head and motioned for Juan to be very quiet getting out. He then motioned for Juan to tie the boat to the tree closest to him.

Once complete, Juan was able to walk a couple of steps up the embankment and waited for Giuseppe. Painfully as he was stepping out, the dingy drifted just enough that Giuseppe fell halfway into the water and Juan ran to pull him out. The wool duster in just those few moments absorbed enough water that it added almost ten more pounds but felt like twenty as the wetness seeped through all his clothes.

The commotion created so much noise that the Police drew their weapons but couldn't see what it was and initially thought it might be an otter, but the Captain in charge disbursed three of his men to investigate and they quickly left on foot to the area.

Frantic, Juan and Giuseppe began running on the embankment as Giuseppe started cursing how cold he was.

In the dark they had no idea where they were headed, only that they were heading towards their car.

When the cops found the boat, they signaled to the Captain, who then radioed the Commodore. He in turn called Sam to alert him.

Sam then radioed the cop waiting by the guys car and told him to be vigilant.

Saratoga Springs
Chapter 18

Rachel and Drake were unaware of the night's activity other than what they were doing. Time passed slowly for the once upon a time almost lovers. Rekindling some affection even after all these years took them down memory lane. It brought them to this very moment in time as they looked into each other's eyes and inspected their mature bodies with pleasant assessment.

Rachel was the first to speak. "DB you still have it!"

Drake chuckled and said, "It gets harder each year to stay in some sort of shape. Age doesn't wait for anyone and my old wounds sometimes reminds me of how much I've been through, but enough of me. You are so stunning, just like the first time we met."

Rachel smiled blushingly and said, "It's been a long time. Go slow DB. I need to relish every moment."

That night, they both enjoyed each other's company and love making. It was old and new at the same time. In the morning all they could do was smile at each other and promised to repeat the evening when his job was all done.

Back at the lake, the two goons continued to trudge through the trees and bushes on the bank. They never heard the State Police following behind them and slowed down their trek as they moved closer to the bridge that would take them back to their car.

Giuseppe was shaking so much his teeth were chattering and he kept muttering beneath his breathe. In the dark light, Juan continued to look back him as the color in his partner's face began to change.

Fifty yards down the path they could see the bridge in the darkness as it appeared like a shadow from an old time movie. Juan stopped and waited for Giuseppe. He was almost frozen as his cheeks began to look white even in this night darkness.

Juan asked, Giuseppe, "Are you good, can we make it?"

Giuseppe replied, "Just keep moving otherwise we are done for."

Just then Juan heard a noise which startled him and as he turned to look at the deer, it ran off and he slipped off the bank right into the river. He was now more soaked than Giuseppe who couldn't reach him to help him out.

Juan cursed like crazy but was able to climb out of the water onto the grass between the bushes. Standing there he tried to ring out as much of the water from his clothes including the wool coat. He knew he was in trouble now and that hyperthermia would settle in quickly if he did not dry off. He quietly said to Giuseppe, "We've got to go now, otherwise neither of us will make it."

With that the two men began slugging through the bushes.

When they finally reached the bridge both men were almost in dire straits. Frozen and chilled to the bone, they were unaware of the police right behind them and on the other side of the bridge.

As they began to cross over on the wooden planks, Giuseppe looked at the far end of the bridge and saw several shadows and knew that it was over.

Juan hearing the branches break behind him saw the police walking right up to them.

Succumbing to the capture, the police Captain was yelling for blankets and hot tea as the officers moved the two men into the police truck.

The Captain in charge then called the Commodore who called Sam to tell them that the men were captured and would be brought to the station for arraignment.

This part of the case was now closed, or at least the police thought.

Across town the following morning, in the Mansion on Clinton St, Mr. Stein called Bill Williams to inform him that Ashley had been found and was safe in his house. He also told him that he would be bringing her home shortly.

Bill of course had many questions but wanted to wait till Ashley was home and, in his arms, before asking them.

When the doorbell rang, Bill opened the door to find Ashley smiling and in tears with Mr. Stein standing behind her.

After entering the house, Ashley hugged her Dad who said to her: "Daughter, I am so happy that you are safe and home. I need to talk to a minute with Allen. Go relax. I will be with you shortly."

Mr. Stein was standing there with a sheepish grin as he now faced Bill.

Bill turned to Allen and asked, "How, where was she and how did she end up at your place?"

"Bill" replied Allen. "I can't tell you all the particulars, just that my son had done this to, in his mind, to protect me and Doris. His actions were misguided by someone outside of his own family who he thought was leading him correctly."

Allen continued. "Needless to say, I found out where this information was coming from and have put a stop to it and was able to figure out where she was, along with Danny, who was by this time in the same situation as Ashley."

"So what you are telling me", Bill interrupted, "was that Danny had taken directions and instructions from someone other than you in his abduction and that you have taken care of the situation?"

"Exactly, yes, that is what I am saying", replied Allen.

"But how?", asked Bill.

"Allen smiled and said, "Let's just say that some of my associates are not happy with so called friends up here and they all stepped in to help find Ashley and Danny."

Bill was thankful and told Allen so.

But Allen, turned to Bill and asked, "I need for you to let this go, regarding Danny. There is no reason to further an investigation or ask any more questions concerning this matter. It is over and I only wish for you and your

Daughter to go on with your lives as my family will. Is this okay with you?"

"Sure", Bill replied. "Whatever you say, as long as I have your word that nothing else will happen to Ashley?"

"You have my word Bill", replied Allen.

But after Allen left Bill was still wondering what really happened and why Ashley was taken in the first place.

However, for the moment he let it go, happy that she was still alive and home safe.

Saratoga Springs
Chapter 19

Night had become day once more and Rachel untangled
herself from Drake as he tried to hang onto her. They
smiled at each other and tried to hold on to that special
moment for just a little longer. But they both knew they
needed to face whatever was in store for them on this
renewed day.

Rachel ran to the shower, saying out loud, "That will have
to hold us for now. I've got a job to do and so do you."

"Can I shower with you?" replied Drake.

Rachel, said, "Nope, it would only prolong the inevitable,
our world at large…"

"Okay", the old detective quipped and got ready for his
turn in the shower.

Back to his business on hand, before leaving the hotel,
Drake asked Rachel to keep close tabs on Nunso, as he
headed to the station.

By the time he arrived, Sam was all smiles, which surprised
Drake since Sam rarely smiled.

"Good Morning Sunshine", asked Sam. "How was your
evening?"

"Mine was great thank you", replied Drake. "Why all the
smiles?"

"Well" Sam answered. "We have the two goons locked up
after they burnt down the Stein boat. Of course, we still

have to question Allen and Doris. And based on what you reported, we are very close to ending this case."

"Not sure I entirely follow you?" replied Drake.

Sam then said, "You told me that Nunso had taken Danny and Ashley to the Stein house after rescuing them, right?"

"Yes, but…" replied Drake.

"That said", Sam began, "means that all parties were saved and that other than a misdemeanor or federal offense, depending on how you look at it, to hang on to the kid, and a First Degree attempt by the two goons we are pretty much done here. I spoke to Bill this morning and he isn't pressing any more charges. In fact, he asked me to back off now, which I told him I would."

Drake responded to Sam with, "Something still stinks and I am not sure what it is just yet. So I wouldn't be hatching all my eggs just yet. I want to know who Nunso is and where does he go from here."

"Ah, I think you are reading too much into this DB", Sam replied. "The case is pretty well locked up."

"All the better for me to hang around and dig a little deeper, if that's Ok with you?"

"Sure", answered Sam. "Just keep me posted."

"I will", Drake said and decided to drive back to the hotel.

Walking into the lobby, Drake saw Rachel and asked to use her phone. Sitting in her big boss chair, smiling at Rachel, Drake called Bill.

Drake and Bill had been close friends during the war, but afterwards they grew apart because Drake played hardball around town as a cop and occasionally had a run in with Bill and some of the investigations of fires and such.

It wasn't that they were on different sides, just that their approach to the cases sometimes crossed each other's path that leant itself to some animosity. Drake thought, "More than likely this is why Bill never called him when Ashley went missing."

Drake asked Bill if he could come over and speak to him and Ashley regarding the abduction. Bill thought it wasn't necessary, but Drake persuaded him that there was much to discuss, since he was convinced that Bill knew from the start what the real story was all about. Drake told Bill, "I'll be there at 3 PM."

Upstairs in his room, Nunso was betting on the ponies and watching the latest college basketball game when he decided to visit the Casino, so he could place additional bets on races that weren't being televised.

He thought it would be a good time to meet with Sonny, so he could devise his plan to eliminate him since he was the instigator behind Danny's haphazard abduction.

Nunso only knew of Sonny from what SA and Allen had told him. And based on that information it seemed that he wasn't all that smart.

Nunso believed "If it hadn't been for Sonny's connection to Boston and a relative of the boss, he probably would have never been in the Springs.

Around 1:30, Nunso got to the Casino and went straight to the off track betting salon, where it was crowded with locals and tourists alike watching the monitors and occasionally screaming at the winning results.

Of course, there were other men and women alike looking in disgusted demeanor as they threw their tickets on the floor after each race.

Nunso wanted to meet the man in charge and asked for Sonny. In response, the pit boss in charge of the racing area, told Nunso that "he was busy", but would be notified that he was waiting to see him.

After about a half hour, Nunso asked the pit manager again to see Sonny. Politely the manager told Nunso that he was not available.

This time Nunso had enough and grabbed the manager by his collar nearest to his Adam's apple and said, "Listen up, just take me to him!"

The manager shaking replied, "Yes Sir. Follow me."

Into the back area of the Casino, the manager walked quickly with Nunso right behind him as they walked down a few corridors finally reaching the offices.

When they burst into the room, Sonny who seemed to be in the middle of an argument with Moe, was about to say something and then saw Nunso standing behind his pit boss.

Sonny, surprised, and really in shock, said, "Mr. Francisco, I am truly sorry, I didn't know it was you waiting to see me. You can go, Salvatore", as the pit boss took his leave.

Nunso smirked and replied. "Geez, I was just coming to place a few bets. Didn't know I had to go through Fort Knox to get to you?"

Sonny apologetically replied, "Again I am sorry. We had some business that we needed to take care of, right Moe?"

Moe, who had sat down across from Nunso, replied, "Yeah, that's right. Some business with Tampa. You know. When you are talking to SA, he comes first. So I am sure you can understand that, right Alphonso?"

Nunso, sensing some hostility, decided to back down, since he didn't want to match trouble with trouble with SA. In fact, he quickly saw that the two hoods were in the driver's seat for the moment and that SA would back them first without knowing the whole truth. So Nunso then said, "Sure I understand. Business first."

The complexities that existed in Saratoga with the two racetracks made for unlikely bed partners. In fact, Sonny and Moe were trying to outdo each other and would gladly rid themselves of the other, if they could. But here they were all buddied up to Tampa, with SA believing that all could be forgiven and business would be as usual.

Yet, Nunso acting as the solo enforcer here, basically for Allen, and without any authority from Tampa or elsewhere knew that he had to play this out so that he was not caught in the middle.

A professional chess player, Nunso knew that he needed to plan out his next five moves with precision to avoid any fallout.

"So", Nunso started, "I still need to place a few bets if it's not too late?"

Moe looked at Sonny, who was nervously playing with a letter opener on his desk and then both started laughing out loud.

Sonny, replied, "Oh sure sure, let me call down. What and where do you want it placed and how much?"

Nunso acting like a humble servant replied, "I'd like to go back to the pit to see the outcomes first."

"Right" replied Sonny and called out front for one of his men, who escorted Nunso back to the Casino area.

When he was gone, Moe checked the door to make sure of it, then turned to Sonny and said, "He's playing us that son-of a bitch. I can feel it. Besides he never mentioned anything about Allen or the girl or anything. He knows something. And who invited him up here. SA never said anything to us about him being in town?"

Sonny knew what Moe was saying and had no answer for him except., "Let's call SA and ask him if he knew why that 'wop' is up here! I wouldn't trust him even if SA told me to do so."

Winning a small amount on a basketball game between Duke and Penn State, Nunso casually strolled through the Casino taking in the layout of the place. He knew where Sonny hid out now through the maze of corridors and figured that there were a few of his guys stashed away in these hallways, laying low in case of trouble.

Walking to the cage by the slots, Nunso cashed in his winning receipt and was paid the $1800.00.

He then went to the bar to have a drink and continued his surveillance of the floor. He noticed where and how many emergency exits there were. Four in total with double doors and no chains.

The main entrance had double doors with five steps leading up to them from the pit.

Compiling his thoughts, he knew that a diversion was needed to get Sonny into the main floor where Nunso would walk him out in the chaos.

Nunso further figured that he would take Danny and Sonny to Canada with him and let his associates decide what to do with Sonny. Danny on the other hand would work for them at the distillery until it was time for him to return to the States.

Back in his office, Sonny and Moe called Tampa on the speakerphone. Hearing that Nunso was in Saratoga, infuriated SA. He knew that there could be some trouble before it was over since Nunso usually worked alone and not necessarily on anyone's orders.

SA replied with "Who the hell invited him up there?"

Moe chimed in and said, "Neither of us. But it could have been Allen, since we hear that the Ashley girl is back home and your guys, Giuseppe and Juan, had been apprehended by the State Police."

"Christ" said SA. "What the hell else could go wrong?"

Sonny spoke up, "What do you mean?"

SA replied, "The Feds are breathing down my neck, so I have to maintain some sort of calmness. I am not sure if this phone call is not being bugged by the Hoover rats."

"Jesus" said Moe. "Okay we will try and keep everything as is and make sure that Nunso slides back to Tampa without any more incidents.

SA satisfied with the conversation said goodbye,

Sonny and Moe then worked out a deal to put their differences aside and work on getting Nunso out of town.

First, they needed to go have a conversation with Allen.

Saratoga Springs
Chapter 20

Not knowing the arrangement between Allen and Nunso,
the two Racetrack owners went to Allen's house to discuss
Danny and Ashley and of course Nunso.

Upon arriving, they were directed into the study where
Allen and Danny were waiting for them. Moe was first to
speak.

"Allen, we are concerned that you had someone come up
here to change our plans regarding Danny and the girl.
Why?"

"You've got to be kidding, right?", responded Allen. "How
in the hell would I let you kill my own son and Ashley, the
daughter of the man in charge of the Families horses? Do
you think I am nuts or are you guys just crazy?"

"Listen", responded Sonny. "We thought in the best interest
of all parties that something had to be done. Unsuitably it's
created more of a shit storm with Tampa and Miami. So
we just need to know what Nunso is up to, so we can
squelch anymore hard feelings and get back to business.
You do know why all of this was done?"

Allen, staring Sonny straight in the eyes said, "Of course.
But trust me no one in the Springs wants this to go any
further and if I were you two, I'd be careful!"

Moe looking totally surprised replied, "Are you threatening
us?"

Just then the office door opened and in walked Nunso and said, "No but I am. So unless you don't want to see the sunrise tomorrow, I'd leave now."

Sonny a bit shaken, said politely, "Listen Nunso we meant no harm. We were just trying to cover ourselves because of what the girl had found and what her old man knew."

Nunso, cracking a peculiar grin said, "Be gone. Let's not discuss this again. It's over. Got it?"

Moe and Sonny shook their heads, turned and walked towards the main door, as the butler let them out to their car.

Danny never spoke but was ready when Nunso said, "Allen, they won't bother you again. Business will be like normal and Danny, I will be by in a few days to take you to Canada. Be ready and make no mistake, this is the best for all."

Nunso then slipped out the office door into another room that took him outside. He watched the two goons pointing fingers at each other and then got into their car to leave. Nunso then drove to the hotel and decided to call SA himself in Tampa to discuss any and all options.

On the other side of town, Drake was driving to Bill's house. He remembered it as if it was yesterday when his wife passed away and the wake was held after the funeral.

Bill owned a large piece of property that had once belonged to his wife's grandfather and went from generation to generation. Each time it was donated to the next set of descendants that normally changed something about the land. Sometimes it was farmed with animals. Sometimes with grapes. It was never the same.

Now with just Bill and Ashley, he rented the land to be used as horse stables. Ironically some of the stables housed Syndicate owned horses that complicated matters not just for him but also for Miami, Tampa and Chicago organizations.

Drake was unaware of the situation until that day. He thought that everything was on the up and up when in reality it was grey.

As Bill and Drake conversed about the abduction and the farm, DB was beginning to understand the web that had been created, that seemed to include everyone in town. Somehow even if you didn't know it, you worked for the Syndicate.

Drake wondered if Sam was included in this accord.

Leaving Bill's that afternoon, DB was unsure what direction he should take regarding Nunso. Bill seemed content with the outcome since his daughter was back safe and sound. Sam seemed content since he had two goons under lock and key. And yet, Drake kept thinking that there was more to the story.

After getting back to the hotel he asked Rachel to send up a white board and some markers. He wanted to write out everything he knew, large enough to see if there were connections and what needed yet to be done. He hoped that after seeing the whole thing in front of him that he would find the answers he was looking for.

On the board that night DB was able to sketch out all the players and what they knew, owned or controlled:

1. Bill kept the Syndicate horses in his stables - looked the other way and was paid for it.

2. Moe controlled the racetrack that Sonny wanted to control. Reaching an agreement, was willing to sell it but only if the price was right.

3. Sonny owned the Casino and harness racing and wanted more control over where the money went, which included eliminating Allen's fees.

4. Allen laundered all the money in and out of town for the Families and was in no way at the moment replaceable or willing to step down.

5. Ashley uncovered a plan for the Syndicate to reap more benefits and money within the town by burning down buildings and buying up the land.

6. Danny was just a loose cannon, unsure and vulnerable to whomever whispered in his ear last.

7. Nunso was hired by Allen to clean up any mess. Did this include Sonny and Moe?

8. Tampa and Miami were trying to keep a lid on the situation without the Feds stepping up their own investigations into the Syndicate's businesses.

Concluding that it was strictly business for The Syndicate and that certain players in the group knew nothing of the other, it was reassuring to Drake that Sam was probably not included.

Thinking to himself, Drake realized that it hadn't change much in Saratoga since he retired.

The Miami and Chicago Families controlled much of what the town did and wanted to keep it that way. The problem was that Tampa seemed to want more and was willing to step on some toes of fellow families to do just that.

Drake knew that he needed to remedy the situation by somehow getting Sonny, Moe and Nunso out of the picture first, even though Allen was the pivot guy. Allen would fall in line once the others were out of the picture.

Concluding that he should tail Sonny and or Moe, Drake drove to the Casino first, then to Allen's since he couldn't find Sonny's car. Unaware where they might be, he then drove back into town where he spotted the Ford with its special license plate. Pulling over next to the curb, Drake decided to wait to see what they were up to.

Oblivious to Drake that Moe and Sonny were really pissed off at Allen and Nunso, they had decided on their own that they would handle the problem and kidnap Ashley again and put an end to any problems in the Springs. They felt that Bill would keep his mouth shut or else he would be dealt with in the same way.

Before Drake could do anything, it looked like a repeat abduction for Ashley except that this time there were two older Jewish guys pushing her in the car. She knew them from her Dad's association with them. Before she could say anything, they had placed tape over her mouth and tied her up, placing her in the back seat with Moe.

Sonny and Moe had driven up to the coffee shop where Ashley was working and had asked her to come outside with them as they had to tell her something about her Dad.

Ashley feared that something terrible had happened to him and asked Dave to take over her shift. It was just after 6 at night, dark and cool outside as she followed Moe with Sonny behind her.

Once outside it was only a few moments before the tape and rope were applied to her. She never got a word out.

Drake couldn't believe what was happening as he peeled away from the curb to catch up with the Ford.

The two men, not realizing that they were being followed by Drake drove more than the speed limit as they crossed over the railroad's tracks heading outside of town.

The Plymouth Drake was driving was gaining on Sonny's Ford and it wasn't until they reach the mountain road to Prospect Mountain, that Drake was able to overtake their car.

When they all started to round the curve to go up into the mountain, Drake floored the engine and quickly stopped in front of them at an angle.

The Ford was trying to stop without hitting the Plymouth as it reach the curve and drove slightly upwards onto the side of the road into the sycamore bushes of a tall tree.

The two men had gotten thrown around as the car came to a complete stop and the engine stalled. Bumping her head, Ashley had slid onto the floor of the vehicle and was unconscious.

Sonny was coming to, when the door opened and Drake pulled him out and punched him so hard, it knocked him out. Walking to the other side, he saw that Moe was bleeding from a superficial wound and looked like he was knocked out.

Drake took each man out of the Ford, dragging them to the Plymouth, then tying them up, placing them in the back seat of the car with tape over their mouths.

Walking to the Ford, Drake opened the back door to see Ashley looking at him with pathetic eyes. He smiled at her as he bent over to pick her up out of the crevice in the car.

Just as he was about to do this, she screamed as best as she could when Moe slammed his fist into the back of Drakes head.

Bewildered by the blow, Drake was stunned and couldn't move for a moment, then with all his force jumped backwards into the heavyset man.

Moe stumbled backwards almost falling over as Drake turned and with his full might ran into him toppling both men over and rolling down the bank onto the road. Moe was staggering when Drake took both arms, clasped his hands together, raising them and smashed Moe in the face as he brought it down in full force in a karate chop move.

Moe fell to the ground and was out cold this time.

Drake didn't know how he had gotten out of the rope.

After dragging Moe back to the Plymouth, he saw the knife that was open on the seat next to Sonny who was wide awake and frightened, by the sight of Drake.

After placing Moe back in the car, Drake went back to untie Ashley.

Taking the tape off her mouth, she asked. "Are you alright? He hit you pretty hard."

"Oh yeah", smiled Drake, as his head began to ache.

Walking Ashley back to the Plymouth, she looked at the two men, now sleeping in the back. She wondered why would they have wanted to hurt her?

Drake said, "Don't worry, they won't hurt you anymore. They will be gone a long time for their actions."

Ashley smiling at Drake said, "Geez I hope so. I was beginning to think that I was Win, Place or Show for these hoodlums. All I ever did was look at some papers. What do I know and who cares?"

"Yeah well", Drake started to respond.

"My Dad is the one who made the deal with Mr. Stein. I just went along with it. Why Sonny or Moe thought otherwise was badly mistaken. Of course Danny is to blame also. He listened to these idiots. They told him that he was golden and that they would bring him into the group and make him a partner. Sonny and Moe were playing the Tampa and Miami people against each other, making them believe that the two were at each other's throat over the racetracks. When they were in cahoots with each other. I heard it all and that's why they probably wanted to keep my mouth shut."

In a matter of minutes, Drake got the whole story. It wasn't just about the papers Ashley had found, it was also about the two men taking over the operations in Saratoga. Allen would have been on the list to eliminate as well. It all now tied together.

When the Florida Families were found out, they would have had to answer to Chicago on why things went sour and who was to blame.

Chicago was mainly Italian. Tampa Italian and Spanish. Miami Italian and Jewish and Boston mostly Jewish. Now there would be a lot of finger pointing, and probably some bodies placed in cement over this fiasco.

Drake didn't care much for politics in either the Families or the law. He really just wanted to try and keep the peace and then go back to his little world of sun, beach and sand.

After the two men were locked up, Drake called Bill to tell him that he was driving Ashley back to the house.

Bill apologized profusely for not telling Drake about what he had gotten himself into.

Drake was a little sympathetic but not too much. He was appalled that the Fireman Chief had waivered in his ability to keep good and bad separate. But this was for Sam to figure out, since Drake was just a retired civilian.

Bill had known from the start the situation. He farmed his land out to be used by the Syndicate. It was a way to insure his and Ashley's safety after she uncovered the truth regarding the intention, and money to control the town. It placed the Syndicate forefront on almost everything.

Now, with the arrest of Sonny and Moe, finally Bill could divest himself of such a deal and return to a normal business, free from any entanglements.

Saratoga Springs
Chapter 21

In finding out the status of Sonny and Moe, Nunso elected
to let the police dispose of the two hoodlums. It would be
less for him to worry about. He now focused on Danny,
since he still needed to take him to Canada to get him out
of the limelight.

Allen was still unsure of this Danny's arrangement but
decided not to go against Nunso and clearly understood the
ramifications if he was not moved north out of the way of
the law.

It was dicey no matter what but Nunso was in charge and
with or without the blessing of the various Families, Allen
went along with the plan.

At that time, there was so much pressure from the
government to shut down all of the Syndicate's connections
in Saratoga and in Florida that everyone concerned were
trying to cover their own asses in the process.

Three days after Sonny and Moe were arrested, Nunso went
to Allen's house to collect Danny. Lots of tears were shed
by son, mother and father. There were promises to be
good, listen to his elders and to not be a hot head in the
process.

Nunso could not say how long it would be before Danny
would return but assured his mother and father that he
would come back provided he was the perfect guest in the
Canadian operations.

Canada was famous not just for its whiskey and maple syrup, but also for the other side of Niagara Falls, Bacon and of course Ice Hockey.

Danny was going to work in one of the many whiskey factories that the Canadian Family controlled.

During Prohibition, booze came from Canada into the States and made most of the Families in the States wealthy beyond belief.

The Speakeasies and Casinos were pouring more alcohol than even before the law went into effect. After the end of Prohibition, the booze flowed just like before, only this time there were legal and illegal barrels floating down Lake Erie into the States, primarily into Buffalo, Toledo, Detroit and Cleveland. Then it was disbursed nationally.

Leaving the Mansion, Nunso, who thought of himself as shrewd and uncatchable, did not notice that Drake was following him in a dark blue colored Plymouth.

The almost six hour trip they would drive, took them down the back alleys of town to route 90 west. Nunso drove the Dodge as Danny occasionally would try to make light of their travels.

Drake had informed Sam prior to tailing Nunso and Danny that when he got the chance he would call and notify him of where he was and what was happening.

The two cars travelling away from The Springs in late afternoon soon encountered a frightful Canadian ice storm that in the early evening placed the traffic at a snail pace on the normally busy highway.

The drive to Syracuse usually took three hours, but six hours later, tired of the storm and slushing snow, Nunso passed the exit for Tyre, then saw the sign for Geneva.

Deciding to spend the night there instead of chancing the rest of the drive in the dark, Nunso took Exit 42 and drove into town. There he found the first motel available, "Allstate Motel".

Drake who had followed them painstakingly through the day into night waited till he saw them come out of the office and walk along the outside corridor of rooms to room 17.

Cold, hungry and hoping that there might be some food in the Motel, Drake drove into the motel parking lot and he slipped into the office and asked for a room.

"Man, you are lucky", the young man of maybe 22 replied. "You are getting the last room, room 15. Must be the storm, we are packed tonight. That'll be $23.90."

"Thank you", said Drake. Then he gave him a $25.00 and told him to keep the change.

Drake then asked, "Is there any food around here or diner that is still open?"

"That's funny", the young man answered, "The two guys right before you came in asked for the same thing. Say you aren't travelling together are you?"

"Must be coincidence". Drake responded.

"Right", said the young man. "Right next door is the diner but closes in about twenty minutes or so, you better hurry!"

"Thanks", Drake replied, got his key and headed directly to the diner. But as he opened the door to go in, someone behind him grabbed the door which made him turn around.

It was Nunso and Danny, looking straight at him.

Since neither had ever each other before, or at least he thought, Drake thanked his lucky stars as he heard Danny say, "Thank You."

Walking into the diner, the waiter asked, "Three?"

"No thank you", came out of Nunso's mouth before Drake could say anything.

Drake just smiled and said, "I'll sit at the counter. Thanks."

After his meal, Drake left before Nunso and Danny, promptly returning to his room. Through the drapes he carefully kept an eye on the walkway to make sure that Nunso and Danny walked back to their room. It wasn't long and Drake then decided he would turn in for the night.

Calling the front office, he asked for a 5 AM wake up.

After calling Sam to tell him where he was, he sat there mindlessly watching T.V. for a bit. This didn't help, and it was still early for him, not quite 10 PM, but he went to bed anyway to get himself rested for what the next day might offer.

Back in room 17, Danny said to Nunso, "I think I know that guy we bumped into in the diner, but I am not sure from where?"

Nunso, cocked his head and said, "Danny don't be paranoid. I would have known if something was up. Your Dad would have told me, since nothing goes on in town without his knowledge."

"Okay", replied Danny and the two me went to bed.

Dawn was peeking through grey skies in the East as Drake dropped off his key and walked into the diner. It was almost 6 AM and Nunso and Danny were finishing their breakfast.

Realizing that they might leave before he even had a cup of coffee, Drake ordered up toast, jam, peanut butter, juice and a large cup of coffee to go. He figured that it would be the best he could do on this early morning drive.

No sooner than he ordered his meal to go, Danny and Nunso paid their bill and walked out to the parking lot and slid into their car.

Drake was tapping the top of the counter as he turned to watch the Dodge pull out of the driveway. He hadn't realized he was annoying the customer next to him, when the trucker said, "Do you mind?"

"Oh, sorry. I was daydreaming", said Drake as the breakfast bag was placed next to him.

After paying for the food, Drake almost sprinted to his car jumping in and sped out of the Motel's driveway, heading for the highway.

The bright sunlight behind Drake's car throw shadows into the still darkness going west on the highway. It was almost an hour before he caught up with Nunso and Danny.

Drake didn't know what Nunso had up his sleeve or where he was taking Danny but knew that it had to be somewhere protected by one of the Families.

Drake's call to Sam last night didn't divulge anything new and so he was going to have to wing it when the time was right.

It bothered Drake a bit that Sam was disinterested about going after Nunso. Granted he hadn't committed a crime and Bill didn't press charges against Danny, so why was Drake even following them?

It seemed that it was the right thing to do, according to Drake. A matter of principle that any person could abduct someone else without consent and by force, without legal consequences.

Drake's ire about the town looking the other way because of the Syndicate's money and influence infuriated him all the more. This is why he retired. He just got tired of chasing the bad guys only to be released by the Police Chief or the Judges.

The drive was pleasant enough with the temperatures climbing into the high 30's, with plenty of sun. By the time they reached the Town of Tonawanda, Drake had an idea where they were headed.

Route 90 turned into route 190 to Niagara Falls.

Drake thought, "From there, Nunso could cross over into Canada."

Deciding to keep up the pace, Drake knew that he was going into uncharted areas once they got into the country. He would have to be extra careful how he played his hand.

Route 190 crosses over the Niagara River into Canada. The border patrol of Canada welcomes you with suspicion anyway, but on this particular day, they stopped every car and made each of the driver and passengers exit for a full inspection.

Drake was three cars behind Nunso, when he got to the border gate.

The entry guard asked Nunso to exit the car politely. Apparently, he was argumentative and the guard called over another officer who then told him something that upset him more. By this time there was a line of cars way behind Drake as he marveled at the amount of attention that Nunso and Danny had acquired.

There were now five officers with guns drawn demanding that the two exit the vehicle. When they finally got out of the Dodge, both men were handcuffed and marched away by the Mounties. Meanwhile a tow truck was lifting the Dodge up onto a flatbed getting ready to tow it away.

Just then, Drake realized that he did not have his own passport and knew that the police would take him away if he caused any problem, so when it was his time to drive up, he pulled over to where it read visitors without paperwork and went into the office.

Behind the counter sat an old old friend from the police academy and Viet Nam, Sergeant Norman Freeman.

Norman was a black athlete who had been in the Olympics when he joined the Canadian Army and spent almost two years in Nam. Younger than Drake, he looked to be in his middle forties by then and in picture perfect shape.

Norman was reading the riot act to Danny and Nunso as he looked at Drake, then smiled.

Standing six foot four, he towered over Drake, but once he saw him, he walked around the two hoodlums, which scared the other police officers in the office, and grabbed Drake.

"Drake, you old son of a gun. How the hell are you? And what the hell brings you to my neck of the woods?"

Smiling at each other Drake asked Norman if they could go into the back room to discuss his appearance.

Norman said, "Absolutely, I need a coffee anyway and we can catch up. Besides these two knuckleheads are getting into my country!"

Saratoga Springs
Chapter 22

Still standing in the lobby, Danny said to Nunso, "I knew I
knew that guy!"

"What do you mean", Nunso said.

Danny replied, "My Dad told me that Sam had asked an old
friend to come up and help him with some stuff. This had
to be the guy. He's been following us since we left town.
He must be a cop or something?"

Nunso, normally the stalker, felt like he was out of his
league this time. He didn't know who Drake was or even
why he was on their tail. But he knew that he needed to get
on with his task at hand and pleaded with the other officers
about his godson.

"Listen' he said, "I need to get my godson to his Father's
house in St Catherine. You can follow us there if you need
to. Can I get like a day pass or something that would allow
us to go there and back? It is an emergency."

The officer was polite and said, "Sit down, I will speak
with the Sergeant when he comes back."

In Norman's office, Drake explained the situation of the
two hoodlums and what had transpired in The Springs.

Norman said to Drake, "Well I can keep them here for the
disruption for a short time. Or I suppose I could call the
locals on your side and have them arrested but it's a bit
flimsy at best, since they really haven't done anything yet."

Drake understood what Norman was saying and they really only had two options. One, the one that Norman just described or two, just let them go into Canada and see what would transpire.

Drake now knew that his cover was blown and that they would be looking out for him, so the best option he could come up with was to have them picked up by the State police and returned to Saratoga for questioning.

Norman told Drake that he understood and they walked back out to the lobby, where Norman spoke to one of his men in private.

Danny was mouthing off about the wait until Nunso told him to "shut up."

Drake knew that he would have to return to the Springs as well and asked one of the officers if he could use a phone.

In one of the back offices Drake called Sam and explained what had become apparent and that he would be heading back shortly.

Sam told Drake that he would contact the State Police and have the two men escorted back as well.

It took about two hours to arrange everything and for the State Police to arrive. When they did, Danny and Nunso knew that they weren't going to Canada after all and would be returning to where they had started.

Upon getting their vehicle released from impound, the State Police took Danny and Nunso outside and told them to get back in their car. After only a few miles of following them the State Police veered left onto another parkway, leaving Danny and Nunso to continue on by themselves.

As it turned out, when Sam called in to the State Police office, the Lieutenant on duty was "friends" with Mr. Stein. Meaning that he was paid by the Family indirectly for monitoring and keeping members out of trouble.

Neither Sam nor Drake knew this.

Drake thinking that everything was on the up and up sat in Norman's office and called Rachel to check on her.

Norman who was finishing the paperwork after releasing the two guys to the State Police, said to Drake, "If you are not in a hurry, maybe you should take some time and drive the long way down through the Falls. It's a sight to be seen on this side during the winter, with the ice cycles hanging off of the Falls is pretty amazing."

Drake smiled and said, "You know Norman, I've never looked at it from your side so perhaps I will. I am not in too much of a hurry to get back especially since the Troopers have the 'boys' in their possession. Thanks, I will take the drive down and spend the night."

Drake then bade Norman farewell and promised to catch up later and began to drive back to Saratoga.

Unknown to Drake as he drove south on 190, a Dodge began to follow him.

Driving to Stanley Ave towards the Clifton Hill area, Drake could take the Rainbow Bridge across to the U.S. side.

Traffic was light especially in the winter but as he merged unto the Niagara Parkway the black Dodge came out of nowhere and slammed into his Plymouth that caused it to forge forward to the edge of the side of the road. Drake was now in a dangerous position inside the car leaning towards the Falls.

Looking over his shoulder there were no lights or cars going in either way, except for the taillights of the car that pushed him. Not getting a good look at it he had no idea who it might have been since he was sure that the State police had Danny and Nunso.

Now in a precarious situation, he knew that if he attempted to move towards the back of the car it might cause the car to either stay put or go over the side into the Falls, so for the moment he tried to keep calm.

Waiting for anyone to go by and see his predicament, he sat in the car for what seemed to be hours.

Fortunately for Drake, the winds coming off the Falls were his saving grace, keeping the car teetering but without moving an inch either way.

Traveling the same road, driving home from his shift, Norman lived in Table Rock just passed Horseshoe Falls, which is the main Falls in the Niagara area. As he drove round the curve to the town his eyes caught a glimpse of something hanging over the side. Slamming on his brakes he stopped in the middle of the Parkway and jumped out of the car running to the side. There he saw his old friend with a daunting smile on his face.

Norman yelled as loud as he could, "Drake, I'll get you out, stay put!"

Running back to the car he opened the trunk and gathered up the cables used for towing and hitched them to the front of his Jeep. He then ran back to the Plymouth and gingerly slung the cables over the bumpers. Once that was done, he attached one additional cable to the underbelly of the car in case all else failed.

Drake turning his head kept checking on what Norman was doing. Then he heard Norman yell again.

"Drake, I am going to back up the Jeep to pull the car up and away from the edge. Got it?"

All Drake could do was give him the O.K. sign with his right hand facing backwards.

It took Norman and the Jeep much more than patience as he slowly moved the Plymouth back from the edge. At one point the right bumper began to come off, so Norman had to stop and bring another cable from the trunk, which was the last one and attached it to the back right axel.

Norman feared that if he pulled too hard that the back end of the car would snap off and the car would drop into the Falls, so he eased the Jeep in reverse, even with an occasional horn blasting from an oncoming car.

After an hour or so, the Plymouth was finally back on the side of the cliff. In spite of the balmy 13 degrees cold night air, Drake had perspired through his clothes and was drenched from the nerve wracking event.

Norman, his savior, said to him after they both unleased the cables, "Come to my home tonight. We both need to have a few."

Drake couldn't agree anymore. This close to death was not the first time, but it certainly was the closest he had been in a very long while.

That night after a few drinks and a few follow up calls, Norman and Drake figured out what happened and who was responsible for the hit on Drake.

Calling Sam, Drake woke him up and explained what took place and that he was Okay thanks to Norman. But his concern was what happened to Danny and Nunso.

Sam assured Drake that he would get on it straight away, but that Drake should get back as soon as he could.

In the morning Norman had his mechanics look at the Plymouth to see how much damaged it sustained. When they were done, the unmarked police car, actually only had the left side of the car damaged that was bent in, along with the right bumper. The axels, tires and underbelly managed to endure the impact of the accident and tow.

Norman told Drake to check out the car that Nunso and Danny were in to see if it was damaged, when he returned to the Springs. And with that they parted ways and Drake told him he'd be in touch.

Saratoga Springs
Chapter 23

Nunso told Danny that a change of plans were now in place
and that they would head back to Saratoga before driving
up into Nova Scotia to get into Canada.

All Danny could say was that he was happy that they took
care of Drake.

Nunso was not as happy, since he was now tied into the
cops not just in Canada but in the Springs as well. This
could mean more trouble than it was worth it. Nonetheless,
he too was relieved that he didn't have to worry about a
tail.

When Nunso drove back to The Springs, neither he nor
Danny knew that they would have a police team waiting for
their arrival.

After conversing with Drake, Sam arranged for the local
police and the State Troopers to hide until the two men
arrived. Sam was inside the Stein house, along with several
other officers, in case Danny decided to contact them.

It wasn't too long after the incident in The Falls, that the
Dodge with the smashed in right fender drove up and into
the Mansion round about.

Just as the men exited the vehicle the whole place sprang
alive with lights blaring and police of all sizes popping up
with guns drawn.

Stunned the two men stopped moving as Sam and the State
police Commander came outside with Mr. and Mrs. Stein.

Sam read the statement…" You two are placed under arrest, anything you say will be…"

Doris and Allen just looked at Danny and could say nothing.

Nunso was fit to be tied that he had been caught up into this trivial incident. He'd have to contact someone in Florida to get him out of this situation.

The local police took Nunso into custody and led him to a van, while Danny was placed into a secure unpaid by the Syndicate, State Police Jeep. After all Danny had abducted someone, which is a Federal offense and still had to pay for that offense.

Both Allen and Doris were also placed in a local police car to be taken down to the station for questioning. Sam hadn't gotten all the facts straight so he was tired of playing cat and mouse with Allen and decided to squeeze him and his wife for the truth.

Returning to the Springs several hours after the arrests, Drake went straight to the station to get caught up. Once he was there, Sam filled him in on what Nunso was hired for, at least from Allen's statement. Doris knew very little except that she knew Nunso and why he was there. All she wanted was to safeguard her son.

In the end Nunso pleaded a no contest for hitting a car and leaving the scene of the crime and was free to leave on his own accord. The problem with it was it occurred in Canada's jurisdiction and so the police had to let him go since he hadn't committed any crimes, per se, in America.

Drake was pissed but couldn't do anything either and so he went back to the hotel, where he slept for ten hours.

After all the drama, Rachel and Drake spent a few days together, promising to see each other soon. Sam went back to the normal small town life and Bill and Ashley began running their horse farm for the locals and a few New York City tycoons, divorcing themselves from the Syndicate.

The Stein couple got away "Scott Free" and continued their businesses as laundries for the Five Families: Chicago, Miami, New York, Tampa and New Orleans.

In spite of trying to clean up Saratoga by the city council, there seemed to be the underbelly of money being paid out to a Family, by someone or some establishment.

Sentenced to five years in New York's Federal Penitentiary Ray Brook, Danny got out in two and a half for good behavior due to a Syndicate bought Federal Judge.

When Drake arrived back home at the end of February, the weather was a welcome treat with the sun shining and 78 degrees. However, there was a letter without a postmark or return address that was left for him. When Drake opened it up, it just read: "The next time I will eliminate you!"

There was no signature, but Drake knew who it came from and just smiled.

For the immediate moment in time, Drake slipped back into his shorts, flip flops and Hawaiian shirt and poured himself a gin and tonic.

"Tomorrow", he said, looking out towards the Gulf, "would be another day."

www.ingramcontent.com/pod-product-compliance
Lightning Source LLC
Chambersburg PA
CBHW030522260626
47157CB00005B/1850